S0-BUD-003

From the Files of
Madison Finn

Read all the books about Madison Finn!

#1 Only the Lonely
#2 Boy, Oh Boy!
#3 Play It Again
#4 Caught in the Web
#5 Thanks for Nothing
#6 Lost and Found
#7 Save the Date
#8 Picture-Perfect
#9 Just Visiting
#10 Give and Take
#11 Heart to Heart

Coming Soon!

#12 Lights Out!

From the Files of

Madison Finn

Heart to Heart

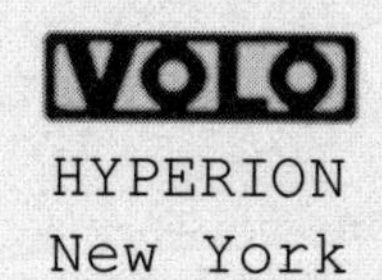

HYPERION
New York

For Rich, with all my heart

Special thanks to the lovely and talented
Lisa Papademetriou

Printed in the United States of America

First Edition
3 5 7 9 10 8 6 4

The main body of text of this book is set in 13-point Frutiger Roman.

ISBN 0-7868-1685-6

Visit www.madisonfinn.com

Chapter 1

"Rowf!"

"I don't know, Phinnie," Madison Finn said as she peered out the living room window. "It looks pretty gray out there."

"Rowf! Rowf!"

Madison's dog, a pug named Phineas T. Finn, barked twice at the window and looked up at her with his big, brown, puppy eyes.

"Okay, okay," Madison said, reaching down to give Phin's head a pat. "I'll get my coat." It was hard to resist Phin when he gave her that look.

"I'm taking Phin for a walk!" Madison yelled down to her mom.

"It's cold outside," Mom called from the kitchen. "Bundle up!"

"Yes, Mom," Madison said, grabbing her rainbow-striped scarf and matching hat.

February air nipped at Madison's cheeks as they stepped outside. The streets were quiet for a Sunday afternoon. Phin barreled ahead like a crazed sniffing machine, little puffs of steam escaping from his nose. Madison waited patiently for him to go through his usual routine, checking out every oak tree on their block. She shifted her weight from one foot to the other so her toes wouldn't go numb.

Sniff, sniff, turn.

Sniff, snuffle, turn.

Sniff, snuffle . . .

Stop.

Phin froze in his tracks, staring straight ahead, brown eyes locked on a golden retriever. Madison couldn't help but stare, too. The retriever was attached to a cuter than cute guy with sandy hair and an olive-green cap tilted on his head.

Phin tugged Madison forward, straining at the leash.

The retriever pulled his owner forward, too.

"Not so fast, Peaches," the cute guy said, keeping a firm hold on his dog's leash. He flashed Madison a bright smile. "Is it okay to say hello?" he asked, indicating the two dogs.

"Meeting Peaches would make Phin's day," Madison said, flashing her own smile.

The two dogs paused and looked at each other

warily; then began sniffing. Phin's bottom wagged and wiggled. Madison laughed.

"My name's Toby," the cute boy said. "My family just moved into the neighborhood. Over on Ridge Road."

"I'm Madison." Madison gestured up the street. "We live on Blueberry Street."

Toby grinned again, and Madison couldn't help noticing how white and straight his teeth were. A hot blush started to creep up the back of her neck, the usual response Madison had in the presence of cuteness. Even though she had plenty of guy friends, Madison still got nervous around certain boys.

"Do you go to Far Hills High?" Toby asked. "I have to start there tomorrow, and I don't know anyone."

"High school?" Madison shook her head. "Uh, no . . . No. I'm in middle school," she explained, flattered that Toby thought she could be older. "Seventh grade, actually."

"Oh, wow," Toby said with a shrug.

"Gee, it's starting to snow," Madison said, holding out her hand.

"Yeah," Toby agreed. The cold wind had died down and now it felt warmer, and faintly icy. Flakes were falling slowly and gently from the sky.

"Well," Toby said.

"Well," Madison said, unable to start up much of a conversation either.

The dogs weren't having the same problem. Phin and Peaches kept right on sniffing and snorting at each other.

"Well, I guess we'd better get going," Toby declared, tugging gently on his dog's leash.

"Well . . . welcome to the neighborhood," Madison said.

"Nice meeting you, Madison," Toby said.

"You, too, Toby," Madison said, loving the sound of his name as she repeated it. He smiled one last time and pulled Peaches away in the opposite direction.

Phin pulled, trying to follow his new, golden girl-friend for a few paces. But he quickly reached the end of his leash. He looked up at Madison and blinked his big brown eyes once again as if to say, "Come on! Let's go! What are you waiting for?!"

Unfortunately for Phin, the look didn't work this time.

Madison's clogs left footprints in the thin dusting of white as she walked the last quarter of a block back to her house. Stepping into the hall, she kicked the snow off her shoes and removed her damp coat, hanging it back on the peg with her hat and scarf. Phin gave himself a good shake, too.

"We're baaaack," Madison said as they walked into the kitchen. Mom was sipping a cup of coffee as she read a piece of paper.

"Hi, honey bear," Mom said, leaning over to give Madison a kiss. "How's the snow?"

"So beautiful," Madison murmured as she looked out the kitchen sliding doors. "And Phin made a new doggy friend." Madison told Mom all about Peaches and Toby.

"A new girlfriend? But Phinnie, what will Blossom think?" Mom asked the dog, chuckling to herself.

Blossom was a basset hound who belonged to Madison's best friend, Aimee Gillespie. Aimee lived up the street, too. Everyone in the Gillespie family joked that Phin and Blossom were "dating."

"Is that for work?" Madison asked, pointing to the piece of paper in Mom's hand.

"Sort of. The *Far Hills Gazette* just faxed this over," Mom said, handing it over to Madison. "They're going to run it in tomorrow's newspaper."

Madison looked down at the page—part of a newspaper layout. In the center of a column titled "TV Top Picks" she saw the very short article Mom had been looking at. Someone had circled it in black ink.

Budge Films Fishes for Success on PBS

Ever wonder how fish sleep, what they do when the surface of their lake freezes over, or what they eat during the long, cold winter? Freshwater, a new documentary developed by the team at Budge Films, has the answers. This two-part documentary was shot entirely on location in the USA.

"A number of people have made documentaries

about ocean wildlife," says Francine Finn, vice president of research and development for Budge Films and senior producer of Freshwater, "while very little has been done on fish and animals that live in rivers, streams, and lakes. These creatures are fascinating. Freshwater is one of our most exciting features to date."

With narrative by Sir Wallace Boyle, Freshwater is a fun, educational film that the whole family will enjoy.

Premieres Thursday at 8:00 P.M. Check your local listings.

"Wow, Mom!" Madison said. "This is great! They even quoted you."

"I know," Mom said warmly. "It's great publicity for the documentary."

Madison nodded. She'd seen *Freshwater* three times already. "I know lots of people will watch it," she said.

"I hope so," Mom sighed, blowing on the hot coffee in her mug.

Madison glanced back down at the paper. It was dated the next day. Below the article, Madison saw the horoscopes and the crossword puzzle.

"Want to hear your horoscope for tomorrow?" Madison asked.

"Sure," Mom said. "Then we can see if it comes true. Look under Leo."

They read it together.

LEO
Monday is a sociable day. Your name will be on everyone's lips, so be sure to project confidence when you walk into a room! If you're not feeling confident—just fake it. No one will know the difference.

"Hmmm, sounds pretty good," Mom said, taking her mug to the sink. "What's yours?"

Madison looked for Pisces. She read the horoscope silently.

PISCES
Love is in the air! But winds that blow in your direction are not from familiar corners. Keep your eyes wide open. Romance will sneak up on you when you least expect it.

"Oh, brother," Madison giggled as she put down the paper.

Mom looked up. "What does it say?"

"It says I'll have a romance," Madison sighed. "I wish."

"Sounds good to me!" Mom said. "Maybe it's that boy you met walking Phinnie."

"Mo-o-o-om!" Madison moaned.

The truth was that Madison only liked one guy,

another seventh grader at Far Hills Junior High named Hart Jones. Unfortunately, Hart had no clue that Madison was crushing on him. When they were growing up, Madison thought that Hart was just a dork. He always chased her and teased her and called her "The Finnster," the dumbest nickname in the history of nicknames. But then he'd moved away for a while. And something had changed when he moved back.

Madison hauled herself up from the chair she was sitting in. "I'm going upstairs to check my e-mail."

"Okay, but dinner's in an hour," Mom said, holding up a can of kidney beans. "We're having vegetarian chili."

"Fine," Madison said. Mom wasn't a very good cook, but chili was one recipe she'd mastered.

Phin's little nails clicked up the stairs behind Madison. He hurried into her bedroom and snuggled in the usual spot by Madison's feet. The computer hummed and beeped as the home page for bigfishbowl.com appeared. Madison checked her buddy list, hoping to find Aimee or her other best friend, Fiona Waters, online.

But as Madison scanned the list of unfamiliar screen names, she remembered that Aimee was at her dad's bookstore and cyber café, helping out. Fiona was with her aunt Brenda, who was in town visiting from California. Neither BFF would be online now.

Madison checked her e-mailbox instead.

FROM	SUBJECT
Bigwheels	Top Secret and Urgent
1800roses4U	Time for Valentine's Day!
JeffFinn	Dinner tomorrow
Orange Crush	<no subject>

She opened the e-mails in order, starting with the message from Bigwheels, her computer keypal. Madison and Bigwheels met inside the bigfishbowl and had been writing ever since. Since Bigwheels lived far away, in Washington State, they couldn't afford to call each other. But they chatted online and sent e-mails all the time.

From: Bigwheels
To: MadFinn
Subject: Top Secret and Urgent
Date: Sun 2 Feb 4:43 PM

I've totally fallen—in love! (BTW: I am screaming this because I am soooo excited.)

There's this way cute guy in math club I've been crushing on. His name is Reggie and he has hazel eyes and black hair and he is SO CUTE!! :)~ NE-way, I never even thought he knew that I was alive,

but today he came up to me and asked me to the Valentine's dance, and I am so excited that I am freaking out! What will I wear? How should I act? Should I talk to him MORE now? Or less? Some of my friends say to play it cool, some say be extra friendly, and I have no idea what 2 do!!

You always ask me for advice. Now I need ur help.

Yours till the math clubs,

Bigwheels

Madison reread the e-mail twice. Wow! Bigwheels never talked about boys like this. How perfect! Madison was dying to tell someone about Toby, the cute guy, too. She'd tell Bigwheels, of course!

She hit REPLY.

From: MadFinn
To: Bigwheels
Subject: Re: Top Secret and Urgent
Date: Sun 2 Feb 5:26 PM

THAT is awesome newz. How could NE guy resist wonderful U? ;o)

Well, I think that you should just be normal and friendly with Mr. Wonderful. He already likes u, so why play it cool, right? HTH

I'm so jealous that you're going to your school Valentine's dance. I don't even know if we're having one! Oh, well. My horoscope said love is coming my way. Maybe if ur in love I will be soon 2? I hope so.

Even my dog Phin's in love. He has a crush on another girl dog we just met up the block this afternoon. They were cute. But the dog's owner was even CUTER. When we started talking he even thought I was in HIGH SCHOOL! Can u believe that? LOL

Good luck w/ur guy. Write sooner than soon and tell me EVERYTHING that happens.

Yours till the puppy loves,

Maddie

After Madison hit SEND, she clicked on the next

e-mail, advertising a sale on dozens of rose bouquets for Valentine's Day.

"Who do I buy these for?" she joked to herself. "Hart? Ha! Ha! Ha!"

DELETE.

She scrolled to the next e-mail. Dad had written, asking if Madison wanted to go out for Mexican food the next night with his girlfriend, Stephanie Wolfe. She'd made reservations for the three of them at Tamales, a new restaurant downtown.

Madison's stomach gave a low growl. It was almost dinnertime. She sent Dad a quick reply saying that she couldn't wait to go to dinner. Madison loved tacos.

Now only one e-mail remained. As Madison clicked on it, she did a double take. Orange Crush? Whose screen name was *this*?

```
From: Orange Crush
To: MadFinn
Subject: <no subject>
Date: Sun 2 Feb 5:13 PM
---
I've got a crush on u.

Your Secret Admirer.
```

Madison stared at the screen, reading and rereading the message even though it was so short. Her heart thumped. Her mind raced. She scrolled up and down, looking for hidden clues.

Orange Crush? Was it like the soda? Or did whoever sent this know orange was Madison's favorite color?

She shifted in her chair, kicking Phinnie in the side by mistake.

"Rowwrooooo!" the dog howled, jumping up to his paws.

Leaning over, Madison picked up Phin and cooed an apology in his ear. "Who sent this, Phinnie?" she asked.

Madison reached for the phone so she could call someone—anyone. She had a secret admirer? This was the kind of news a friend needed to share in person. But then she remembered that her friends were busier than busy.

What horrible timing, Madison thought.

She'd just have to wait to tell Aimee and Fiona about it tomorrow.

Chapter 2

"Do you think it was *him*?" Madison asked, pointing to a supercute ninth grader wearing a leather jacket.

Aimee and Fiona cracked up. The three friends were standing in front of Aimee's locker. Madison filled them in on the mysterious e-mail from Orange Crush early Monday morning. At lunchtime it was still a great mystery.

"The truth is—it *could* be that guy," Fiona said.

"Well, the person has to be someone who knows you well enough to get your e-mail address," Aimee said. "And they must know you like orange."

Madison glanced down at her orange backpack. "Well, that doesn't really narrow it down much. Anyone can see what my favorite color is."

"I bet it's someone you're already friends with," Fiona suggested.

"Yeah . . . like Egg!" Aimee said, giving a quick little twirl. Aimee took ballet, and she usually did dance moves when she got excited, which was pretty often.

"Egg? No WAY!" Madison laughed. Walter "Egg" Diaz had been one of Madison's best friends since they were younger. He was more like a brother.

"Aimee, you don't really think the secret e-mail is from Walter, do you?" Fiona said quickly. "I mean—Walter doesn't like Madison, right? That was just a joke. You're joking, right?"

"Chill out, Fiona," Aimee said. "Of course I'm joking."

"Egg doesn't have a crush on *me*, Fiona," Madison said. She smirked. She knew that Egg was crushing on Fiona and vice versa. Fiona liked Egg so much that she called him by his real name.

Fiona bowed her head a little. "Oh," she said meekly.

Madison and Aimee exchanged looks and smiled.

"Besides," Aimee said with a laugh. "A secret admirer e-mail isn't really Egg's style. He's not really—the romantic type."

"Hmm," Fiona fiddled with one of her braids. "Maybe it was Chet."

"Chet?" Madison shrieked. Chet was Fiona's twin brother. "Oh, please!"

"Fiona!" Aimee yelled. "Chet is the only guy in this school who is *less* romantic than Egg!"

"I know, I know," Fiona laughed.

Aimee shook her head. "Come on, we have to get serious. Now, think. Who are the prime suspects?"

The girls stared at one another.

"Hart Jones?" Aimee suggested.

Madison felt her heart stop. Literally stop. When it started pumping again, it was chugging at twice its normal rate. "H-H-Hart?" she stammered.

"It *could* be him," Fiona said. "He has your e-mail address—right, Maddie?"

Madison let out a nervous giggle. "Yeah, along with practically everyone else in the seventh grade. Why would it be him? It could be Drew or Dan or Suresh, too."

"Yeah, but didn't Hart like you in second grade, or something?" Aimee asked.

Madison snorted. "I think he's probably gotten over that by now." She tried to sound like she didn't care, but secretly she was wondering if Aimee could be right. Was Hart Orange Crush?

Brrrrring!

When the bell rang, the three friends started toward the cafeteria.

"Hey—Maddie! Aimee! Wait up!"

Madison turned and saw Egg jogging toward them, followed by his friends Drew Maxwell, Dan Ginsburg, Chet Waters, and Hart Jones.

Hart!

Madison wanted to hide.

"Hey, Finnster," Hart said, raking his brown hair out of his eyes.

"Hi," Madison said. It came out like a whisper. She looked away, unsure about what to do or say.

"You going to the cafeteria?" Egg asked. He was staring right at Fiona.

"Yeah, we're being lured there by the smell," Fiona said sarcastically.

Egg laughed.

"Mmmmm—mystery lasagna." Chet made a retching noise.

"Suspiciously, lasagna is what they served us last Friday," Dan pointed out. "Coincidence? Or ancient leftovers?"

Madison chuckled. She'd gotten to know Dan better this year because they both volunteered at the Far Hills Animal Clinic. Dan's mom worked there as a nurse, and Dan was an animal lover, just like Madison.

"Indestructible, cardboard lasagna," Aimee said.

"The same batch that's been around all year!" Drew added.

Everyone cracked up.

"What's so funny?" asked a voice behind Madison.

Madison turned around and came face-to-face with "Poison" Ivy Daly—her least favorite person in

the seventh grade. Once upon a time (in third grade), Ivy and Madison had been good friends. But then Ivy transformed into Miss Obnoxious and started hanging out with her two drones, "Phony" Joanie Kenyon and Rose "Thorn" Snyder. When she was elected president of the seventh grade, tensions mounted even more.

Ivy stood there holding a stack of hot-pink flyers. She was wearing a fuzzy pink cardigan sweater that matched.

"I hope I'll see you all at the Valentine's Day dance next Friday," Ivy said, passing a flyer to Hart first. "It's going to be a lot of fun . . . and we're raising money for a good cause."

Madison grabbed a flyer.

Have fun and help fight heart disease at the
HEART TO HEART DANCE!
Who? Everyone! All Far Hills Junior High
students, grades 7–9
When? 8 P.M.–10 P.M. Friday, February 14
Why? All proceeds to benefit the
International Heart Society
Where? Far Hills Junior High Gymnasium
How much? $5 single ticket in advance
$8 for two tickets in advance
$6 at the door, single tickets only
Buy your tickets early and save!

"We're also having a carnation sale next week," Ivy said.

"Carnations? For me?" Chet cracked.

"No, we're having a competition to see who can sell the most. All proceeds from that are going to the Heart Society, too," Ivy said.

Sell the most? Madison thought. She rolled her eyes. She means who will *get* the most. And Ivy will be sure that the winner is herself.

Egg took a few more flyers from the pile.

"Ta-ta!" Ivy chirped. "I hope I'll see you all there!" She gave Hart a flirtatious look and flounced off.

"Ta-ta!" Egg repeated mockingly when Ivy had walked away. He waved the pink pages in the air.

The group giggled.

"Here's what I think," Egg said, folding his flyers into a paper airplane. He held them up and the boys laughed.

"What are you doing that for?" Aimee squealed, prancing in place. "Don't you think this dance looks like fun?"

"Are we supposed to buy carnations for all the girls or something?" Drew asked, looking squarely at Madison.

Chet cracked up. "Yeah, right."

"Do we get dates for the dance?" Fiona asked.

Egg tossed his pink plane into the air. "I like doing *this* better," he said, aiming a plane at Dan's head.

"It says here that it's eight dollars for two tickets

in advance," Madison said, looking down at her flyer again.

"I guess we all DO have to find dates!" Drew crowed. "I want to save the money!"

Hart laughed. "Well, I already know who I want to go with," he said.

Everyone got quiet. Madison felt her cheeks get hot. Was Orange Crush about to reveal himself? Was his date pick . . . Madison? She held her breath.

"I WANNA GO WITH EGG!" Hart screeched, reaching over to give Egg a fake embrace.

The boys all laughed again. Madison sighed. Out of the corner of her eye, she saw Fiona give Egg a sly smile. He smiled back, awkwardly looking down at his shoes.

Madison wished Hart would smile at her, but he was still goofing around with the other guys.

The group started walking toward the cafeteria again, everyone talking excitedly about the dance and the carnation sale. Madison moved down the lunch line slowly. All Madison could think about was Hart. Will he ask her to the dance?

"I know you're a *chip* off the old block, Maddie," Dad joked later that night, "but maybe you'd better take it easy on the chips. You act like you haven't eaten anything all day."

Dad, Madison, and Stephanie were sitting in Tamales, waiting for their food to arrive. The waiter

had brought out salsa and a basket of tortilla chips, and Madison was having trouble resisting.

"I kind of skipped lunch," Madison said as she dipped another chip into the salsa. "It was lasagna day at school."

"Oh, yuck," Stephanie said. "Whenever they served lasagna at my school, it used to make the whole hallway smell disgusting."

Madison laughed. "That happens at my school, too," she said.

Stephanie grinned, tucking a strand of curly dark hair behind her ear. "It's nice to know that some things haven't changed since the Stone Age," she said.

Dad put his arm around Stephanie and squeezed. "I'd hardly call a few years the Stone Age," he said warmly.

Madison's smile faltered, and she looked away from them. Even though she really liked Stephanie, sometimes she felt awkward when her dad and Stephanie acted all lovey-dovey.

Really awkward.

"You look beautiful tonight," Dad said, gazing at Stephanie.

Madison shoved another chip into her mouth. Why was her dad being so extra-gooey tonight? She glanced around the brightly colored restaurant. Cut paper decorations hung from the ceiling, and there was even a live mariachi band.

"I'm going to get the band to serenade us," Dad said suddenly, grabbing Stephanie's hand.

"No, Jeff—" Stephanie protested.

But it was too late. The band had seen Dad wave and was headed for their table.

Madison twitched in her seat. *Serenade?* She wasn't sure she could deal with sitting through an entire song, watching Dad and his girlfriend stare at each other.

"Dad!" she blurted. "I think I'm sick."

It was as though the words had sprung from her mouth by themselves. Madison put her hand to her forehead. She spit a chewed-up chip into her napkin and groaned a little.

"Are you okay?" Stephanie asked, giving Madison a concerned frown. "She looks a little pale, Jeff."

Dad waved away the mariachi band.

"It's my stomach," Madison explained, clutching at her middle. "I think I ate too many chips. Wow, I feel really bad."

It wasn't a total lie, of course. Madison really was nauseated—but from watching Dad and Stephanie.

"The chips? Aha!" Dad said. "See?" He dropped Stephanie's hand and reached for Madison. "Will you be okay?"

Madison mumbled, "I don't think so."

"Should we cancel dinner?" Dad asked.

Stephanie leaned over to Madison. "Do you want to go?" she asked.

Madison shrugged and covered her mouth.

"Why don't we go back to my apartment," Dad suggested. "You can lie down there awhile." He motioned for the waiter and asked to have their food to go.

"Maybe I should just go back home instead to my own bed," Madison said. "I feel really, really bad. I am so sorry."

Stephanie put her hand on the back of Madison's neck. "I'm sorry, too, sweetie. I was really looking forward to our dinner tonight."

Madison felt a pang of guilt mixed in with the nausea. As they got up to leave, she said nothing more. The ride back home was quiet, too, except for a few moans and groans. Madison used those for effect.

When they pulled up in front of Mom's house, Dad helped Madison out of the car.

"Feel better," Stephanie called as Madison hurried up the front walk.

"Yeah, and no more chips for you," Dad joked.

"Thanks," Madison called back. "I'm sorry!"

She waved with a limp wrist and blew a kiss to her dad, who stood by the car, waiting to see that she got inside all right.

"Maddie?" Mom looked up from her book as Madison walked into the living room. "What are you doing home so early? Did you have dinner already?"

"Not exactly. I didn't feel well," Madison said.

Mom frowned and got up from her chair. She put her hand on Madison's forehead. "You don't feel hot. What are your symptoms?"

"My stomach was hurting," Madison fibbed. "But it's better now."

Madison and Mom walked into the kitchen together. Madison grabbed a few cookies.

"Hey! What are those?" Mom asked. "Dinner?"

Madison stuffed one into her mouth and put the others back into the jar on the counter. "Oh. Maybe I'd better just go to bed."

"Hmmmm. Be sure to wake me up if you feel sick in the middle of the night," she said, raising an eyebrow.

Madison gave her a wry smile. "I don't think I'll need to, but thanks." She didn't feel like talking about Dad and Stephanie right now.

Mom understood. "I love you, honey bear," she said, not forcing the discussion.

Madison gave her a kiss and trudged up the stairs. Phin followed right behind as usual. It was only 8:30 and Madison wasn't tired at all. She closed her bedroom door so Mom wouldn't discover that she wasn't really sick (even though she probably already knew that). Then she logged on to her computer, watching as the cursor flashed yellow and the pages loaded. Phin looked up at her curiously for a moment in the half-darkness and then snuggled into a pillow.

Madison opened up a new file.

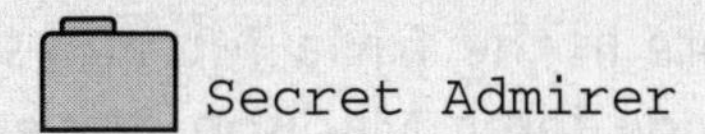

I can't believe I just lied to everyone about being sick. But I just couldn't sit there and watch Dad. I had to do something.

Now that I'm home I feel so badly. I should be happy that Dad is happy, shouldn't I? Especially since he and Stephanie may be in love. And the truth is, Stephanie is nicer than nice. What's wrong with me?

Rude Awakening: If love is supposed to keep us together, why does it always leave me feeling unglued?

I wonder what REAL love is like—the kind that sticks? What is it like to have someone like you that much, someone who you like back? Aimee says she's been in love before. Fiona, too. I bet even Ivy Daly has had real love by now.

I wonder whether my secret admirer could be someone who likes me and who I'll like back?

Where are you, Orange Crush?

WHO are you?

Maddie closed the file and headed onto the Web to play some games in the main tank on bigfishbowl.com. The Web site had a new section devoted

to online games where members competed against one another.

After an hour or more in the Trivia Tub and several games of Beach Bingo later, Madison powered down her computer and crawled into bed. Mom was coming up the stairs. It was nearly eleven o'clock now.

"Maddie?" Mom whispered, poking her head inside the bedroom.

Madison pulled the covers up to her chin, pretending to be fast asleep.

"Good night, honey bear," Mom whispered.

She opened her eyes when Mom walked out, and watched as the shadows on the wall danced in moonlight. Phin was snoring loudly.

Madison wondered what real love was really like—and whether horoscopes could ever really be right.

Chapter 3

Bleep! Bleep! Bleep!

Madison rolled over and smacked the snooze button on her alarm clock. Calculating that she didn't actually have to get out of bed for another twelve minutes, she snuggled beneath her comforter. But she wasn't tired anymore. Thankfully, she wasn't nauseated anymore, either.

Madison thought of getting up to call Dad, but she decided not to do it. *Maybe I will send him an e-mail instead*, Madison thought, throwing off the covers. She jumped up to check her e-mail.

The first message was from Dad.

From: JeffFinn
To: MadFinn
Subject: Feeling Better?
Date: Mon 3 Feb 9:49 PM

Maddie,

Just wanted to check in and make sure that you are okay. You looked pretty green at the restaurant. And I know it's not easy being green.

Love you,

Dad

Madison smiled at the joke but then quickly frowned at her computer screen. She felt even guiltier now.

From: MadFinn
To: JeffFinn
Subject: Re: Feeling Better?
Date: Tues 4 Feb 7:13 AM

Hi Dad.

I'm feeling better—thanks for writing. I still don't feel 100%. Can we make a raincheck o=)

Please tell Stephanie that I'm sorry I ruined dinner.

Love u,

Maddie

Madison pressed SEND and zapped the e-mail into cyberspace. She clicked on a message from Bigwheels next.

From: Bigwheels
To: MadFinn
Subject: RE: Re: Top Secret and Urgent!
Date: Mon 3 Feb 10:02 PM

After I read your Emsg, I decided to give him a call on the phone just to say hi. He was so sweet!!!!!!!!!!! We talked for almost an hour, and he totally made me laff about ten times!!!!!! Reggie is like the world's most perfect guy. He's cute, he's funny, he's smart—I swear, he's like the kind of dream boy that you want to live with forever and ever into infinity!!!!!!!!!! I just hope he likes me as much as I like him. Otherwise, I'll be so sad. (:-...

Okay—have I talked about him enough? I can't stop!

Yours till the wedding bells,

Bigwheels

Madison groaned. Was everybody in the world falling in love—except for her? It seemed that way. She clicked on a file and started to type.

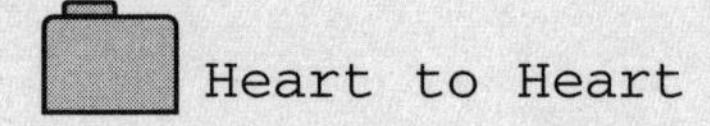

Rude Awakening: If love makes the world go around, why can't it stop in and see me sometime?

The "Heart to Heart" dance is around the corner—and I want to go! And I'm not talking about going alone.

I'm tired of feeling like the love train has just left the station and I'm the only one standing on the platform.

I'm sick of waiting around for the love boat—when it's already sailed.

LOL!!!!

What's so hard about LOVE anyhow? It seems like everyone else I know falls in love at the drop of a hat—or at least they say they do. Why is it taking me a billion

"Madison!" Mom called, breaking into Madison's thoughts. "Honey bear, you'd better hurry up, or you'll be late for school."

Madison glanced at the clock. "Oh, no!" she

gasped. She only had ten minutes to get ready! She'd completely lost track of time.

She hurried to her dresser and pulled out a pair of heavy black leggings and a soft red sweater.

After a quick swipe at her hair with a brush, Madison dashed through the door and down the stairs.

"Hi, Mom," Madison said as she walked into the kitchen. Her mom had already set out a glass of orange juice and a green apple. Madison gulped the juice, casting an eye toward the kitchen clock. "Bye, Mom," Madison said, dropping her glass in the sink.

"Have a good day," Mom said with a grin. "I guess you're feeling better today?"

"Oh. Better? Yeah," Madison said, faking a cough. "MUCH better."

Madison grabbed her orange book bag, which was sitting in the front hall, and stepped out in the crisp, cold air. The sky was grayer than gray, blocking out the sun. Madison bit into the tart green apple.

Two blocks away from the house, Madison spotted a familiar figure crossing the street.

"Fiona!" Madison called. "Over here! Wait up!"

Fiona turned and gave Madison a smile. "Hey!" she said. "Running a little late, aren't you?"

Madison laughed. "Look who's talking!"

"Tell me about it," Fiona agreed. "Chet already left. I was a little slow this morning."

The two friends fell into step toward the school. "Did you oversleep?" Fiona asked.

"Actually, I got up *early*!" Madison said. "I just lost track of time checking my e-mail."

"So . . ." Fiona wiggled her eyebrows. "Any more messages from mystery man?"

"Not this morning," Madison shook her head.

"Hmmm," Fiona said. "Maybe the first one wasn't meant for you."

"Gee, thanks a lot!" Madison said. Both girls laughed.

Kids streamed into the main doors of FHJH. Fiona and Madison blended into the crowd. The first bell had rung. They still had five minutes until the late bell. Madison chomped on her apple and tossed the core into a garbage can near the lockers.

The core hit the floor instead.

"Nice shot, Maddie," Ivy said, walking by at the exact moment when Madison missed her throw. "You should go out for basketball," Ivy added.

Madison bent down to pick up the core as Ivy walked away, hips swaying with attitude.

Aimee saw the pair and hurried over. "Hey, Fiona! Hey, Maddie! What's the update? Any more secret admirer messages?"

Madison shook her head. "No more. And would you keep your voice down, please? You never know who's listening."

"Hmmm," Aimee said. "Maybe Orange Crush is just waiting to see what you'll do next."

Madison tugged open her locker with a huff. A red envelope tumbled out.

"Whoa!" Aimee said. "What's THAT?"

Madison turned the envelope over and over, looking for some clue, but there was no writing on the outside. She tore it open and pulled out a red construction paper heart.

U have a good heart, the note on the inside read. *Signed, Your secret admirer.*

"What does it say?" Fiona asked.

"It's a note from your admirer, isn't it?" Aimee said, pirouetting a little. "I knew he'd do something else!"

Madison read the note aloud.

Fiona peered over at the card. "It's pretty," she said.

"I wonder if whoever made it is still in the hallway, waiting to see what you do when you open it," Aimee said, looking around.

"Maybe it *was* that ninth grader," Fiona joked. "He's over there at his locker again."

"Cut it out," Madison said. The hallway was packed. She stared at all of the familiar faces. For some reason everyone seemed like a stranger today.

Ivy strolled by again with her drones. She cast a glance back at Madison.

Could the secret admirer be *her*? Madison wondered. Is this whole thing just a valentine trick?

Madison studied the note. She tried to remember some old letters Ivy had typed back when they were friends. Ivy would pick print that was very different from this. This note didn't have the loops and

curlicues Ivy had liked. The person who typed this was more formal—more *boy*like somehow.

Brrrrring!

When the bell rang, Aimee said good-bye. Madison and Fiona headed off to Mr. Gibbons's English class, Madison as confused as ever about the identity of her secret admirer. She slid into her seat. Luckily, Mr. Gibbons was too busy writing an assignment on the board to notice their lateness.

"Everyone, please copy down this week's writing assignment," Mr. Gibbons said, pointing to the blackboard. "Instead of having you all do book reports on *My Brother Sam Is Dead*," he said, naming the novel the class was currently reading, "I've decided to give you an independent project instead. You should find a biography or an autobiography, or some other nonfiction book on a person or subject from the American Revolution, and then write a three-page paper on that topic."

The class groaned in unison.

"Good, I'm glad to hear that you're all excited about the assignment," Mr. Gibbons said. "You may work alone or in pairs. The project is due next Friday, February fourteenth. My Valentine's Day gift to you all."

Madison heard a cough coming from behind her. Something small and white scooted beneath her desk. After a moment, she "accidentally" knocked her pen off her desk, picked up the note along with her pen, and smoothed it open on her lap so that Mr. Gibbons wouldn't see.

Maddie,
Let's do a project 2gether! I'll come over later—soccer is canceled 2day!

Fiona

Madison turned in her seat and gave Fiona a thumbs-up.

While other kids in class chose their partners, Mr. Gibbons handed out a sheet of vocabulary words. Then he led the class in a discussion of the last chapter of the book they had read.

Mr. Gibbons was in the middle of a profound thought when the classroom phone jingled. *Cha-ching!* He turned his back on the class to answer it.

The moment he did that, everyone started talking.

"Hey, Maddie," Dan Ginsburg whispered. He was sitting to her right. "Guess who came into the animal clinic yesterday?"

Madison smiled at the eager look on Dan's face. "Judging by your expression, I'm guessing it was someone good," she whispered. "Britney Spears?"

Dan laughed. "Ha-ha," he said. "No. A llama named Gertrude!"

"No way!" Madison cried. Her voice squeaked so loud that a few kids turned around to look right at her, including Hart, who was sitting in the front row.

Madison's heart flip-flopped. Hart had a big smile on his face. She couldn't take her eyes off him.

". . . so *then* the llama needed emergency surgery," Dan said. "Uh . . . hello?"

Madison turned and realized that Dan was still talking, even though she hadn't really been listening.

"I'll definitely have to come by the clinic sometime to see," Madison said.

"See what?" Dan asked.

"The llama," Madison said. She was looking at Dan now, but her eyes kept shifting to the back of Hart's head.

"Maddie, what are you talking about? I just told you that the llama was sent to the zoo for special care," Dan said.

"Sure," Madison said absently.

"Huh?" Dan said, grabbing his books and shoving them into his bag.

"Where are you going?" Madison asked.

"Class is over," Dan said. "Didn't you hear the bell?"

Madison shook her head. She hadn't heard much of anything except her own dreamy thoughts. Hart had smiled at her. Just when she thought that her crush on him couldn't get any worse, it had. It was worse than ever now that Madison thought it was possible—just possible—that he was Orange Crush.

"See you later, Maddie," Dan said as he walked out of the classroom.

"Uh-huh," Madison said.

But she was looking at Hart when she said it.

Chapter 4

"If Mrs. Quill makes us diagram one more sentence," Aimee said, "I swear, I'm going to scream. Loudly." She had been lying on her belly on the floor of Madison's room, poring over her grammar book, but now she flipped the cover closed and sat up. Since Aimee had early morning ballet practice instead of her usual after-school time, she could join Madison and Fiona's study group.

"Fiona and I have a paper to write for our English class," Madison said.

"Who can think about homework when there's a school dance coming up?" Aimee asked, pulling a magazine off the pile on Madison's nightstand. "Let's look at hairstyles," she suggested.

"Great idea," Fiona said, clearing a place for Aimee on the bed. "We can study later."

Aimee giggled and plopped on the bed. Phin jumped down. It was getting crowded up there.

"I want to look good at this dance," Aimee gushed, talking a mile a minute. "The eighth and ninth graders will be there, and I don't want to feel like some seventh-grade baby." She shook her silky blond hair as she flipped through page after page of smiling teen models.

"What are you going to wear?" Madison asked.

"Well, since it's Valentine's Day, I was thinking that I would wear my red velvet dress," she said, "but maybe I should go shopping for something new."

"Yeah," Fiona admitted. "It's the most romantic day of the year, and I want to look *good,* too."

"For your date?" Madison asked, smiling.

Fiona giggled. "Well . . ."

"Well what? Well what?" Aimee asked. "Did Egg ask you?"

"Calm down," Fiona said with a laugh, "nobody's asked anyone anything yet. But Walter and I did have a *very* interesting conversation last night online. He Insta-Messaged me." She fiddled with one of her braids.

"And?" Madison and Aimee asked at the exact same time.

"And I decided that I might as well tell him that I

like him." Fiona's voice was matter-of-fact, but her eyes were dancing.

"Oh my God! You didn't. You did? I can't believe it!" Aimee cried.

"Wow," was all that Madison could say. An image of Hart flashed in her mind. There was no way that she could do what Fiona had done.

"So what did he say?" Aimee asked.

"He said that he liked me, too," Fiona replied.

Madison and Aimee squealed. "NO WAY!"

"Get out!" Aimee shrieked. "Egg said that? I can't believe it!"

"Wow," Madison said. "Does this mean that you guys are a couple now?"

Madison was happy for Fiona, but she felt a teeny twinge. Would all of her friends get dates while she was the only single girl in seventh grade?

Fiona shrugged. "Well, we're not a couple," she admitted. "I mean, we like each other, but we haven't said that we're a couple. He hasn't invited me to the dance officially or anything."

"He's playing it cool," Aimee said, nodding knowingly.

"Oh, please. Since when does Egg know about cool?" Madison asked. "He probably hasn't even thought of asking you."

"Hmmmm. Good point," Aimee said. "*We* should think of it for him!"

"What?" Fiona asked. "You've got a weird 'I'm

planning something crazy' look on your face, Aimee. What are you thinking?"

"Don't worry, I won't do anything embarrassing," Aimee promised Fiona. "I'll just call Egg and *casually* mention the Heart to Heart dance and *casually* mention that Fiona said that she wanted to go and oh-so-very *casually* remind him that it's cheaper for couples to buy their tickets early. . . ."

"No!" Fiona yelled.

"Yes! Let's do it!" Madison said eagerly. She ran to get the portable phone from Mom's room. From his sleeping spot on the floor, Phin yawned, his long pink tongue curling like a ribbon.

Fiona giggled. "No! No! Don't do this!"

Madison handed the phone to Aimee.

"No! NO!" Fiona continued to protest, giggling the whole time.

"Shhhh! Fiona, you have to be quiet, or Egg will get suspicious," Aimee said as she started punching in Egg's home phone number.

Fiona put both hands over her mouth to stop her giggles. Madison put her head next to the receiver so that she could hear as well as Aimee.

After the third ring, someone picked up. "Hello?" said a voice.

Madison made a face. Aimee's jaw dropped and she immediately slammed down the phone.

"What are you doing?" Fiona asked.

"That wasn't Egg. That was Señora Diaz!" Aimee

shrieked. Egg's mom was a Spanish teacher at Far Hills Junior High.

"Oh no," Fiona grimaced.

"I hope she doesn't have caller ID," Madison said. Everyone cracked up.

"Okay, that totally didn't work," Aimee said. "Let's call someone else!"

"And say what?" Madison asked, unable to control her laughing.

"Let's find out who the other guys are asking to the dance," Aimee suggested. "It'll be fun! Maybe *they* know if Egg is asking Fiona . . ."

Fiona huddled toward Aimee eagerly. "Let's do it," she said.

"Who should we call next?" Aimee asked.

"Drew," Fiona suggested.

Madison nodded. Drew was Egg's best friend. "If Drew is asking someone to the dance, Egg probably will be, too," she said.

This time, Madison punched in the number. She had it listed inside her orange address book.

The phone rang twice before Drew picked up. "Helleeeww?" he said in a goofier than goofy voice. Madison felt snickering rise up in her chest—she couldn't control it. Quickly, she clicked off the phone.

"Maddie! I can't believe you just did that!" Aimee said, laughing.

"He—he—he said—" Madison could hardly

speak, she was laughing so hard. "Helleeeww?" she imitated Drew's silly voice.

Aimee and Fiona hooted. Fiona laughed so hard that she actually snorted, which sent Aimee and Madison into even bigger hysterics. All of the laughter put Phin into hyperdrive. He woke up, ran around in circles, and started yapping at his own tail.

"Stop!" Madison gasped. "I have to stop laughing."

"My face hurts," Aimee said, tears streaming down her face. "But I can't stop!"

"THAT was funny," Fiona said.

"Oh, please," Aimee said, calming down. "We can't ask them who they want to go to the dance with. Like they'd tell us!"

"Yeah, no one we know is romantic," Fiona shrugged. "Except for Madison's mystery man."

"Yes," Aimee said, looking at Madison. "I wonder who Mr. Romance is?"

"Take a look at the suspects," Fiona said in an official voice. "Who would have access to red construction paper?"

Aimee and Madison looked at each other for a moment, then dissolved into more giggles.

"Good one, Fiona!" Madison said. "That really narrows it down."

"Who would you really like to go to the dance with, Madison?" Fiona asked. "I mean it. For real."

"Yeah, Maddie," Aimee joined in. "Who would you go with?"

Madison pressed her lips together. Part of her really wanted to tell her friends about her crush on Hart, but she couldn't risk it.

Thankfully, she didn't have to answer. She was saved by Mom.

"Hey, girls," Mom said from the doorway. "Studying hard?" She eyed the books that had been shoved off the bed in a heap.

"We're taking a short break," Madison explained.

"Yeah, really short," Aimee added, laughing again.

"Mmmnuh-huh. Well, I'm about to order Chinese food," Mom said. "So who's staying for dinner?"

Aimee checked her watch. "Yikes!" she said. "I didn't realize it was so late. I should get going. I was supposed to walk Blossom tonight."

"I have to go, too," Fiona said. "This is my aunt Brenda's last night in town and Mom is making a big dinner." She jumped off the bed to gather her books.

Madison drew in a deep breath, relief flooding her body. "Oh, you have to go? Okay," she said, trying to keep her voice even. "I guess I'll see you guys tomorrow then."

"E me later though?" Fiona said as she and Aimee headed out the door. "We still need to talk about the project for English class that we didn't talk about. This wasn't exactly a study group, was it?"

"I'll write or call," Madison promised.

"Let me know if Orange Crush e-mails you again tonight," Aimee whispered.

Madison smiled. "I will, I will! Good-bye."

Mom followed the girls into the hall and waved good-bye.

After everyone had gone and the house felt a little quieter, Madison picked up her pillow and squeezed it against her chest. Was she being disloyal by still keeping Hart a secret from her friends? She had come so close to blurting out her feelings. But if Hart wasn't the orange crusher, Madison thought, how humiliating would *that* have been?

Since she still had a few minutes before the takeout dinner arrived, Madison booted up her computer and started a new file.

If only my Magic 8 Ball were here instead of at Dad's house! Then I could shake it, and find out whether Hart is really my mystery guy. Do the signs really point to yes? Or is that just what I want to believe?

Gramma Helen always says that when things are meant to be, I'll see little signs along the way. But DBEYH! All of the signs I see around me don't seem to apply to my life. I'm looking for a clear sign that says STOP or GO or at least HANG IN THERE.

Rude Awakening: My zodiac sign is

Pisces, but my real sign is: ROAD CLOSED.

It seems like anytime I like a boy, he likes somebody else. Or else he ignores me. The "good" thing always seems to happen for girls like Ivy.

When will the good thing happen for me?

Madison was just about to save the file to her hard drive when an Insta-Message popped up on her screen. Her mouth fell open.

This was a sign.

<Orange Crush>: Hi. I see U R online.

Madison's fingers flew across the keyboard. This was her big chance! She had to find out if Orange Crush was who she thought—hoped—it was.

<MadFinn>: WHO R U???
<Orange Crush>: Someone who likes U. :>)
<MadFinn>: Is this a joke?
<Orange Crush>: No.
<MadFinn>: Then tell me who U R!!
<Orange Crush>: MWBRL. Got 2 go.
<Orange Crush>: *poof*

Madison stared at her keyboard, sighing. "Where did he go?" Madison thought. "I want to know who

you are. I *need* to know!"

But the Insta-Messenger was gone.

Disheartened, Madison reread the chat. Why did he have to leave so suddenly? Was "secret admirer" really just someone playing a joke—or was Orange Crush the real deal?

Madison wondered why she couldn't trust the signs when they pointed in one, positive direction: someone really DID like her.

It was only a matter of time before she found out who it was.

Chapter 5

"Ouch! Phinnie, stop!" Madison said groggily.

Phin ignored her. He marched across Madison's comforter, paws prodding and poking into Madison's tummy the entire time. He finally settled on a spot just south of her chin and north of her ribs.

"Don't get too comfortable there," Madison grumbled, nudging him off to the side. He yelped as she got out of bed, staring at Madison as she slid her feet into her fuzzy monkey slippers and stood up. A light rain tapped gently against the window glass. It was a perfect mall day.

What else was there to do on a dreary February Saturday but shop—or go online? Madison would do both. She collapsed onto her desk chair and booted up her laptop.

The Dance

I feel like time is just racing by. Thursday and Friday were so busy. I helped out at the animal clinic, Mom had a business dinner, and now it's the weekend already. I wonder if my secret admirer will send me another message soon? I haven't gotten anything the last two days.

There's way too much to do before the Heart to Heart dance—my mind is spinning.

1. Buy new dress (+ shoes??)
2. Decide on hairstyle (up, down, or braids?)
3. Nails? (Or no, cuz I will just bite off the polish?)
4. Figure out ID of Orange Crush—VERY IMPORTANT
5. Get Dad to teach me his "cool dance moves" (ha-ha)

I can hardly wait till later to pick out something cool @ the mall. Boop-Dee-Doop just opened up a new outlet store and I am psyched. They e-mailed me a 20% off coupon a couple of days ago, and I've been dying to use it ever since I downloaded it. Here's the deal: Mom and Dad have each given me $30 for a dress, so if I use my coupon, I can probably afford to get some hair clips or tights, too. I need to look perfect. Luckily, Aimee and Fiona are meeting me so they can help me with my look. :-1K-

Rude Awakening: When in doubt, shop.

Can a new outfit make the pre-dance jitters vanish?

It better.

The clock in the corner of Madison's monitor flashed.

"Yeeps!" Madison said, hitting SAVE and closing the file. Time really was flying by. It was 10:15 already. If Madison was meeting Aimee and Fiona at the Far Hill Shoppes at eleven, she had to dash.

"Hey, I'm glad you're up," Mom said from the doorway. "I brought you some breakfast."

"Thanks, Mom," Madison said, hopping out of her chair. She took the glass and plate from her mom and placed them on the bureau. Then she took a bite of the crisp bagel, smeared with cream cheese. "I can't believe how late it is already."

"Yup. You'd better shake a leg," Mom said.

"Give me twenty minutes," Madison said, taking a quick gulp of juice.

"I'll be in my office," Mom said. "Come and get me when you're ready."

Madison nodded and took another bite of bagel as she shut down her computer. She pulled on a pair of faded jeans and her favorite gray cable-knit

sweater. This outfit would be easy to take on and off in the stores at the mall—and Madison wanted to do a lot of trying on.

A gorgeous dress for the dance was in Madison's near future.

At exactly eleven minutes past eleven, Madison was standing where her friends had agreed to meet: the Roundabout. The Roundabout was a rotating sculpture shaped more or less like a tall blob with two heads that was located in the center of a bridge stretching from one side of the second level of the mall to the other. Below was an open atrium space with rows of stores and carts. Above was the food court.

Madison's mom had left her at the Roundabout while she headed into a linens and bath store. They would meet up again at 2:30, which left Madison a few hours to go shopping with her friends.

"Where are those guys?" Madison thought impatiently as she glanced at her watch again. But only a minute had passed. Madison gazed down at people on the lower level of the mall. She leaned out over the railing and saw three girls about her own age. . . .

Ugh.

Madison leaned back and walked around to the other side of the Roundabout. Those weren't three girls—it was one girl and two drones! Of course, Madison expected to see Poison Ivy, Rose Thorn, and Phony Joanie at the mall. With only a week to go

before the Valentine's Day dance, where else would they be?

Avoid lower level at all costs, Madison told herself.

"Hey, Maddie!" Fiona called as she and Aimee hurried up to the Roundabout. "Sorry we're late."

"It's my fault," Aimee explained. "I had an early ballet practice that ran over."

"No problem," Madison said. "I was just people watching. Lucky for me, I saw Poison Ivy down there."

Aimee rolled her eyes. "If only we had some water balloons," she said.

"Hey, look who else is at the mall," Fiona said, pointing to the upper level.

Madison looked up and saw Chet, Dan, Egg, Hart, and Drew walking in single file near the railing.

"Hey, Egg!" Aimee yelled. The boys heard and looked down, pointing.

Chet leaned over the railing like he was going to spit, but he didn't. Dan pretended like he was going to throw himself over the edge, which made the rest of the guys laugh.

Fiona waved to Egg, who waved right back. She pointed to the food court, then pointed to her watch and held up two fingers. Egg nodded, and Fiona grinned.

"What is that all about?" Aimee asked.

"We're meeting the guys at the food court at two o'clock," Fiona explained. "Egg and I planned it yesterday."

"You could have told us!" Madison said.

"What's the big deal?" Fiona said with a shrug.

"I guess nothing." Madison shrugged.

She looked up again in time to see Hart and the rest of the boys disappear toward some upper-level shops.

"What are we waiting for?" Aimee asked. "Let's start shopping!"

The girls headed straight for Boop-Dee-Doop, which turned out to be a major letdown. They didn't have any of the cute things that Madison had liked when she'd browsed their online store.

"Do you like these?" Aimee asked as she flipped through a rack of plaid capri pants.

"Nah," Fiona replied. "Too loud."

Madison held up a purple tank top, which was on sale.

"You can't wear that for like three months!" Aimee yelled. "It's still cold out, Maddie."

As Madison replaced the top on the clearance shelf and they left the store, she felt a small wave of disappointment. Boop-Dee-Doop had no dresses she liked. And now that she wouldn't be able to use her discount coupon, Madison wasn't sure she'd be able to find a dress that she could afford in another store.

"Let's try here," Aimee said, pointing to a sign that read "In the Pink." It was decorated with cute little flowers. Madison had never seen this shop before.

"What—is everything pink?" Fiona asked.

"Who knows?" Aimee said. "But considering that we're shopping for a Valentine's Day dance, that might not be such a bad thing."

The store window was decorated with hearts and flowers, too, and mannequins in long dresses. Just the kind Madison was looking for to wear to the dance!

The minute Madison walked inside the store, she knew she'd found something perfect for herself to wear. In the Pink had clothing in all different colors—not just pink—and it was all priced right. There were dresses and tops and pants and even shoes!

She flipped through a rack of black crocheted tops displayed over red long-sleeved shirts. "Maybe I could wear this, with my long black skirt?" Madison wondered aloud.

"Madison, over here!" Aimee called from the back of the store.

Aimee was holding up a dress in pale mint-green velvet with an asymmetrical skirt. She held it up against her body. "What do you think?" she asked.

"I love it," Madison said. "It'll look great with your hair. Try it on."

"Madison, you should try this one," Fiona said, holding up a sea-blue dress with black trim and long sleeves.

Madison frowned at it. "Actually, I was thinking of getting something in red. . . ." she said.

Fiona rolled her eyes. "It's Valentine's Day," Fiona

said, "and everyone will be in red. Don't you want to be different?"

Madison wasn't so sure she did want to be different. Sometimes it was easier to blend in than stick out. But she took the dress from Fiona anyway, and followed Aimee into the dressing room. They got stalls right beside one another.

Madison kicked off her shoes and stepped out of her jeans. Then she pulled on the dress, which was surprisingly comfortable. Madison hated dresses that clung too close or were made of scratchy fabric, but this one was soft and flowy. She looked in the mirror and smiled. The deep, sea-blue color actually shimmered under the light when she moved from side to side. The dress had bell sleeves and a scoop neck, which made her look taller, too. It looked kind of silly with her heavy woolen socks, but with some pale blue stockings and her favorite black Mary Jane flats . . .

"Are you wearing yours yet?" Aimee asked through the stall.

"Yep," Madison said. "You?"

"Nope. Mine looked horrible, so I took it off already," Aimee said, opening the door to her stall. She had already changed back into her normal clothes. "Let me see yours."

Madison opened the door and stepped out.

"Whoa," Aimee said, her eyes opening wide. "Maddie, you have to get that dress, it looks so great on you."

Just then, Fiona walked into the dressing room holding a long red dress. "Maddie, if you don't like the blue one, I found something else for you to—" she stopped midsentence and gasped. "Oooooh! You look beauuuuutiful."

Madison felt herself blush. "Do you really like it?" she asked.

"No question," Fiona said. "THAT is the dress."

"Fantastic," Aimee agreed. "How much?"

Madison bit her lip as she looked for the tag. It wasn't on either of her sleeves.

"It's in back," Fiona said, pulling at the tag. "Hold still." Her forehead creased as she read the tag. "Fifty-two fifty," she said. "Marked down from ninety dollars!"

"Can you afford that?" Aimee asked.

Madison nodded, grinning. "I'll even have seven fifty left over."

"Enough for lunch with the guys," Fiona chirped. "You have to get it!"

Madison couldn't stop smiling as she changed back into her clothes and paid for the dress. She kept picturing herself at the exact moment when she would walk into the Heart to Heart dance. She would be the envy of all the other seventh graders as she danced around the gym with Orange Crush.

Even Ivy would have stop and stare.

That was the best part.

* * *

"Okay, so what do we want?" Fiona asked as she gazed up at a sea of choices on the food court menu. "Burgers, noodles, pizza—"

"Roma Pizza Oven," Aimee said quickly. "They have the best veggie pizza."

"Sounds good to me," Madison agreed, and the three girls headed over to the counter to order slices and sodas.

"There you are," said a voice behind Madison.

The girls turned to see Egg, Chet, and Hart. Madison caught her breath.

"Hi," Madison said. She looked down at the floor to avoid making eye contact with Hart. She wondered if he could tell that she'd been daydreaming about him all morning.

"Hey, Finnster," Hart replied matter-of-factly. He said hello to Aimee and Fiona, too.

"Drew and Dan nabbed a table for us," Egg said, pointing to the far end of the food court.

"Great—we'll join them. And I'll save you a seat," Fiona said flirtatiously as she grabbed her tray.

"Oh-oh-okay," Egg said. He was blushing and stuttering at the same time.

"Actually," Hart said uncomfortably, "I sort of promised Ivy that I'd eat with her." He nodded in the opposite direction from Drew and Dan, where Ivy was camped out with her drones.

"Way to go," Chet said, giving Hart a thumbs-up. "She looks cute today."

Hart stifled a laugh. "Yeah, whatever. I promised, that's all."

Madison had to control herself from making an ugly face. She glared over at Ivy's table. When Ivy saw Madison looking in her direction, she gave her a tight little smile.

"Sorry, you guys," Hart apologized as he walked away.

"No big deal," Dan said. "We'll catch up with you later."

"Yeah," Madison agreed, still masking her disappointment. "See you later, Hart."

He smiled at Madison again, and she felt dizzy. It was probably her good luck that Hart was going to eat with Ivy, Madison thought to herself. If she had to sit down next to him during lunch, she would have been so nervous that she probably would have ended up with half of her pizza in her lap.

Madison, Aimee, and Fiona took their trays and headed toward Dan and Drew who had staked out a big, round table.

"What's up?" Aimee asked as she slid into the seat next to Dan. "Buy anything good?" She nodded at a small brown bag on the seat next to Dan. He'd loaded up his tray with two hamburgers, a super-size container of fries, and a large drink.

"A couple of CDs," Dan said, popping a french fry into his mouth. "But the guy at the record store

clearly thought my taste was less than cool. What does he know? He had both eyebrows pierced and a blue mohawk." Dan imitated the look on the guy's face, pretending to sneer at Aimee's pizza.

Drew started to laugh so hard that he actually let out a snort.

"But you bought the CDs anyway," Fiona said.

Dan shrugged. "Do I care what that guy thinks about my taste in music?" he asked. "I mean, he didn't ask for my opinion on his lame haircut."

Chet slid into the seat next to Madison.

Egg plunked his tray onto the table. "Hey, Drew, slide over," he said.

"Why?" Drew asked, clearly confused.

Egg gave Drew a look, then glanced quickly in Fiona's direction.

"Oh," Drew said, running his fingers through his spiky hair. He slid over so that Egg could sit next to Fiona.

Chet rolled his eyes and Madison hid her smile behind a napkin. Clearly, she wasn't the only one who was still getting used to thinking of Egg and Fiona as a couple.

"Are you going to have that?" Dan asked Aimee. Half of the giant chocolate-chip cookie she'd bought to go with her veggie pizza was sitting on her tray, uneaten.

"Are you kidding?" Aimee asked, eyeing Dan's tray. It was almost empty, of course. He had already

devoured his hamburgers. Only a couple of fries were left.

"Aim, I never kid about food," Dan said, lifting the remains of the cookie off of her plate and taking a bite. "Mmmm!" he said, grinning.

Madison smiled. Dan was a big guy—taller and wider than any of the other boys in the seventh grade. When they were in fifth grade, some of the kids used to call Dan Pork-O. But Dan never really seemed bothered by it. Madison really admired his confidence.

"Hey, Dan," Egg said. "Come with me to get some ice cream."

"Ice cream," Dan said, his eyes dancing. "I won't say no to that!"

"I'm coming, too," Chet said. "Anybody else want some? Fiona?"

"Yeah, Fiona," Egg said. "Want some ice cream?"

"No, thank you, Walter," Fiona said, smiling.

Chet punched Egg in the shoulder. "Thank you, Walter," he said under his breath.

Madison and Aimee exchanged looks. Was Chet as weirded out by this new boyfriend side of Egg as the rest of the group was?

"Anyone else?" Dan asked. "Going once . . . going twice . . ."

Everyone said no, they didn't want anything, and the guys headed off to the soft-serve counter, leaving the girls alone with Drew.

"Dan is so funny," Aimee said once the guys were

out of earshot. "He's the cool, funny kind of guy I always wanted to have as a brother."

"You've got three brothers already," Madison pointed out.

"Yeah," Aimee agreed, taking a sip of her soda. "And none of them are cool or funny."

"So, Fiona," Drew said in an oh-so-casual voice. "Are you going to the Heart to Heart dance with anyone yet?" Fiona looked shocked, and Drew added quickly, "Egg wants to know."

Madison looked at Aimee, and they both laughed. Egg hadn't asked Fiona to the dance yet because he was chicken! He had Drew do his dirty work for him.

"Tell Egg that I'm totally free," Fiona said.

Drew smiled. "Who are you going with?" he asked Aimee.

Aimee shrugged. "You, Drew!" She laughed out loud.

"Very funny," he said. "What about you, Maddie?"

Madison gulped. She glanced over in the direction of where Hart was sitting with Ivy and the drones and then looked back to Drew. "No one," she said.

Drew took a deep breath, like maybe he was going to say something, but then he was interrupted by a flying napkin.

"Gotcha!" Egg wailed, running back over to the table.

The boys had returned with their ice cream cones. Egg elbowed Drew and Drew gave his friend a nod. Chet smacked Egg on the back so hard that it almost sent his waffle cone flying. Egg slid into the seat beside Fiona and sighed.

"Want some?" he said, offering his cone.

Fiona shook her head. "No thanks." She grinned at Madison.

Madison wanted to gush and celebrate her friend's date, but she just couldn't. Her smile back to Fiona felt forced.

It wasn't that Madison wasn't happy for her friend. She was. But couple stuff was hard to get used to. When junior-high couples were strangers you saw from afar, holding hands in the hallways at school . . . *that* was okay. When they were your friends . . . it was way weirder.

Madison checked her watch. "Ooopsie," she said. "It's three fifteen. I have to meet my mom soon."

"Same here," Aimee said.

"Actually, I'm supposed to call my mom," Fiona said. "But maybe Chet and I can ride home with you, Maddie?" Fiona asked.

"Sure," Madison said. "Does anyone else need a ride?"

"Could you drop me at the animal shelter?" Dan asked.

"No problem," Madison said. "Drew, what about you?"

"I'm meeting up with Hart later. Egg and I are going home with him," Drew said. Madison nodded. Drew and Hart were cousins.

The friends said good-bye, and Madison headed to the Roundabout with Fiona, Chet, and Dan.

"Hey, I'll . . . um . . . talk to you later . . ." Egg said to Fiona before racing off after Drew.

Aimee gestured as though she was typing to Madison, who nodded. They would e-mail each other later.

When Maddie, Fiona, Chet, and Dan arrived at the Roundabout, they were still a few minutes early. The boys headed toward the music store. Madison and Fiona flopped on a bench. Madison looked at her bag from In the Pink beside her. She couldn't wait to get home and show Mom the dress.

A funny Valentine's Day window display caught her eye. And Madison dragged Fiona to investigate. A beefy mannequin was wearing boxer shorts with lipstick kiss marks on them and sunglasses in the shape of hearts. On his head, he wore a pair of Bobblers with hearts at the ends of the springy antennae. "For Phinnie!" she said, and rushed in to buy them.

While Fiona checked out some lipsticks in the front of the store, Madison stared out into the busy mall.

Was that *Dad*? She squinted. It sure looked like him, standing at the counter in a store across the mall. The man shifted slightly, so Madison could see his whole face. It was him!

Just as she opened her mouth to shout, "Dad," a salesman walked up to him. Madison backed off. The salesclerk was handing Dad a small black box.

She glanced up at the store sign.

Jewel of the Nile.

A jewelry store? What was her dad buying? Madison swallowed hard. The little black box looked like the kind that rings came in.

Like engagement rings . . .

"Oh, wow," Madison told herself. Dad would never propose to Stephanie without telling me first. Would he? She hesitated a moment, watching, waiting to see what her dad would do. Her dad smiled at the salesman, nodded, and shook his hand. Madison backed away so fast that she bumped into someone on her speedy retreat.

It was Fiona.

Madison jumped. "Sorry," she said quickly.

"No problem," Fiona said, "I didn't mean to sneak up on you." She looked closely at Madison. "Are you okay?"

"I'm fine," Madison lied. "Well, not really but . . . I'll tell you later."

"We should go meet your mom now," Fiona said.

"Right," Madison said. "Let's hurry, then."

She and Fiona double-timed it toward Mom, Chet, and Dan. Madison had never been so happy to get away from a jewelry store in her life.

Chapter 6

<Bigwheels>: Maddie, RU there? U haven't replied to my emsgs in days
<MadFinn>: sorry about that. I've just been a little stressed
<Bigwheels>: what about???
<MadFinn>: saw my dad in the mall day before yesterday. OMG he was in a jewelry store
<Bigwheels>: so?
<MadFinn>: It looked like he was buying a ring.
<Bigwheels>: what kind?
<MadFinn>: Like maybe he's going to ask Stephanie to marry him

<Bigwheels>: R? Did U actually see the ring? Was it definitely an engagement ring? Did U ask him about it?
<MadFinn>: no—I just ran.
<Bigwheels>: but u don't know 4 sure
<MadFinn>: No . . . but why else would he be in a jewelry store?
<Bigwheels>: IHNI. Maybe he was getting earrings for Valentine's Day. Or maybe something for U!
<MadFinn>: I didn't even think of that . . . that would be so cool. A ring 4 me! Should I ask him about it?
<Bigwheels>: Do U really want to tell him U were spying on him??
<MadFinn>: Good point . . .
<Bigwheels>: Maybe u can find out another way. Ask him what he's getting Stephanie for Valentine's.
<MadFinn>: :>:)
<Bigwheels>: Guess what Reggie gave me already? A silver heart necklace. He said he couldn't wait until Friday to give it to me
<MadFinn>: That's so sweet! Listen, I've GTG. Major project to finish

in English—I'll be up all nite
if I don't start.
<Bigwheels>: Okay. E me. TTYL!

Madison sat back in her chair and sighed. She hadn't really planned on working on her English project. That was just a convenient story to get out of the Insta-Message chat with Bigwheels. But now that she thought about it, Madison pulled out her reading materials to make an outline. The paper was due on Friday—only four days away.

Hearing a squeak, Madison turned to see Phin munching on a bright orange chew toy in the shape of a carrot. The carrot squeaked with each bite, which only made Phin attack it more, slurping and snuffling excitedly. Madison smiled. It was easy to make her pug happy.

"Why isn't it as easy to make *me* happy?" Madison wondered to herself, turning back to her computer.

She began jotting down a few ideas for the paper. Then Madison clicked on the bigfishbowl.com search engine, to see what it came up with. She typed in the words *American Revolution* and clicked on the first site that popped up.

If you want to participate in a
reenactment of any of the major
battles of the American Revolution,

please contact the Society for Better Understanding of the Revolutionary War. The American Revolution was a time of great struggle, but it was also a time of great innovation. . . .

That page gave Madison another idea.

What would it be like if she and Fiona wrote about Revolutionary War generals for their presentation? She typed *George Washington* into the search engine next. It brought up a Web page about the first presidents of the United States.

George Washington faced many challenges upon his inauguration as first president of the United States.

Madison scrolled down to a passage about the second president.

John Adams struggled with his role both as vice president and during his time as the second president of the United States. As we can see clearly in his letters to his wife, Abigail Adams, who urged him to "remember the ladies," John was concerned both with social . . .

I wonder what John and Abigail Adams's letters were like? Madison wondered. Would they be as gushy as Bigwheels's letters about Reggie? Somehow, Madison doubted it. She bookmarked the Web page so she could mention it to Fiona. Maybe they could even look up historical letters online?

There were so many ideas. Madison left the search engine and opened her e-mailbox.

There were no letters in her mailbox, but just the thought of Hart writing one sent Madison's mind churning. What would he say? What would she say back to him?

If only.

Madison shut down her laptop and decided to call Aimee. She went into Mom's room, snatched the cordless off of her nightstand and flopped down on the bed. Phin jumped up beside her and rolled over on his back, wiggling, his paws in the air.

Madison punched in Aimee's number and waited as the phone rang.

"Hello?" It was one of Aimee's brothers.

"Hi, it's Madison," she said. "Is Aimee there?"

"Oh, hi, Madison, it's Doug." Doug was in ninth grade. "Can I have Aimee call you back later? I'm watching the basketball playoffs right now with a friend."

"What does that have to do with being on the phone?" Madison asked.

"He's at his house, I'm at mine," Doug said.

Madison sighed, glad that she didn't have brothers who hogged the phone for no good reason. "Okay," Madison said. "But you will give her the message, right?"

Time for plan B, Madison thought as she punched in Fiona's number. The phone rang three times. "Hello?"

"Yeah? Who is this?" the voice on the other end said.

Madison groaned. It was Chet—another annoying brother foiling her plans to get in touch with her friends!

"Hi, Chet," Madison said, trying to keep the irritation out of her voice. "Is Fiona there? It's Maddie."

"Hey," Chet said. "She's here, but I'm on the other line. Can she call you later?"

"Who are you talking to?" Madison griped. "The president of the United States?"

"Why do you want to know?" Chet asked.

But Madison was too annoyed to stop now. "I mean, you're just talking to one of your stupid friends, right?" she barked. "Why is your phone call so much more important than mine?"

"Stupid friends?" Chet asked. "They're your friends, too!"

Suddenly, Madison heard a click on the line. Someone had picked up an extension. Good, Madison thought, I'll tell Fiona to kick her dumb brother off the phone. "Fiona, I—"

"Hello?" said the voice.

Madison gulped. She'd know that voice anywhere. And it sure wasn't Fiona's.

"Hart, I'm still on the phone," Chet said. "Do you need to call your mom?"

"Yeah, sorry," Hart said. "I thought you were done."

"No problem. So, Maddie," Chet went on in a superior tone, "if you don't mind, my *friend*—" he put extra emphasis on the word, "needs to use the phone now."

"Finnster?" Hart said. "What are you up to?"

"H-h-hi, Hart," Madison stammered. Suddenly, she couldn't think of another word to say besides "Bye!" as she slammed down the phone.

"What have I done?" Madison moaned to herself. She fell backward on the bed. "If Hart is my secret admirer, why can't he just come out and say so?" she screamed.

"Rowrowrooowr!" Phinnie howled.

Madison propped herself up on her elbow. "What is his problem, Phin?" she asked. "I mean, even Egg is admitting his true feelings. Why can't Hart?"

Phin looked at her, then trotted to the door. He turned back and stared at her. "Rowroooo!" he barked.

"Oh, I get it," Madison said. "Walk time."

She trudged downstairs and pulled on her coat, then clipped the leash to Phin's collar. She called out

to her mom that she was taking Phin out, then stepped into the chilly evening air.

Phin put his nose to the ground and snuffled. After a moment, he was tugging on his leash like crazy.

Madison laughed. "Whoa, Phin! Slow down!" she said, but he ignored her.

She let him lead her down the block and around the corner, not really caring where they went through the purplish twilight. After three blocks, Phin strained hard against the leash, snapping Madison back to reality. What was Phin so eager to get at? Madison looked up, and saw the answer headed straight for her.

"Hi, again!" Toby called. "Whoa, Peaches, slow down!"

The glossy golden retriever pulled at her leash, and Toby hurried to keep in step. Madison chuckled to herself. Phin's curly little tail was moving so fast that it almost wagged into a blur.

"It's Madison, right?" Toby said, flashing his same white smile.

"Yeah, hello, Toby," Madison said shyly. "How's high school so far?"

"Good," he said, pushing his shaggy blond bangs off of his forehead. "Everyone here is nice."

"Rowrooooooooof!" Phin barked as Peaches nuzzled him happily.

"I hate to break up this romantic moment," Toby said, "but I've got a ton of homework."

"Same here," Madison said. "I guess I'll see you around."

"I think the dogs will make sure of it," Toby joked. "Bye, Madison."

Madison gave Toby a little wave as he steered Peaches away. Phin gazed sadly after her for a while, then looked up at Madison.

"Really, Phin," Madison said, pretending to scold him. "You should at least try to play hard to get once in a while, don'tcha think?" Phin blinked up at Madison, and she laughed. "Come on, let's go home."

Reluctantly, they headed back to Blueberry Street.

"Mom—where are you?" Madison called as she unwrapped her scarf from her neck and hung it on the peg in the hall along with her heavy jacket.

"I was in my office," Mom said, walking into the living room as Phin dashed to the kitchen in search of dinner. "But then the doorbell rang and I got this."

Mom was smiling from ear to ear. In her hands were a red envelope and a red rose. The rose was wrapped in red tinfoil at the end. It was made of chocolate. "Look what arrived while you were out!"

"Wow," Madison said, sighing. "Someone must really like you, Mom."

"Not me," Mom said, handing the envelope and rose to Madison. "It's for you."

"No way!" Madison said. "Did someone bring it over? Huh? HUH?" she asked eagerly.

Mom shrugged. "I don't know," she said. "Whoever it was rang the doorbell and left before I answered it. These were on the mat outside."

Madison ripped open the envelope and pulled out the card. It had a picture of a bear on the front, holding a red paper heart. She read the message inside.

Happy Valentine's Day in advance.
signed, Your Secret Admirer

"A secret admirer, huh?" Mom asked, grinning. "Is this the same guy you were talking about this weekend?"

"Yeah," Madison said. "Kind of." Her head was spinning. Orange Crush was totally Hart. She knew for sure now. He had been around the corner just moments ago, at Chet's house. And he had spoken to her on the phone, so he knew she was home, too. It had to be him!

"Any idea who it is?" Mom asked. "I had no idea seventh-grade boys could be so romantic," she added, winking.

"I've got to go call Aimee," Madison said quickly.

"Dinner in an hour," Mom called as Madison dashed up the stairs to her room. "Don't get all wrapped up online, okay?"

Madison took the steps two at a time up to her room.

IT WAS HIM! Madison thought as she punched Aimee's number into the phone. She hoped that neither Doug nor any of Aimee's other brothers would answer again.

"Hello?"

Madison grinned. It was Aimee! "Aimee, it's me," she said in a rush. "You said to call when I got another message from my secret admirer and I got one. I GOT ONE!"

"What did he say?" Aimee asked.

"It's more than just a note. It's an early Valentine's Day card and a chocolate rose!" Madison said. "I've never gotten a rose before!"

She had to hold her receiver away from her ear as Aimee squealed into the phone. "That is so totally romantic!" Aimee shrieked. "I'm coming right over!"

"Okay, see you soon," Madison said, hanging up the phone.

She leaned down and lifted Phin into her lap.

"Wawoooo," he whimpered when she squeezed too hard.

"Oops, sorry Phinnie," Madison said, kissing his wet nose. She felt a whoosh of adrenaline inside. She could hardly sit still.

She had her first rose.

She would have a date for the dance.

And she would finally—*finally*—get the chance to tell Hart Jones how she really felt about him.

Chapter 7

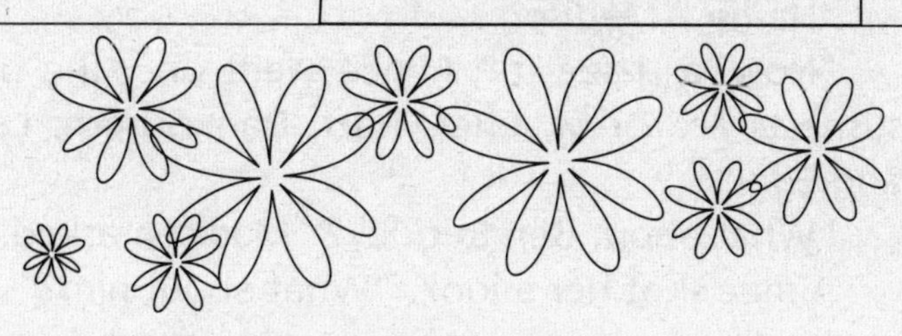

"Okay, Maddie, we've got to get serious about this," Aimee said as she folded her legs Indian style and leaned forward to type something on Madison's laptop. "If we really want to find out who Orange Crush is, we'll have to look at all of the evidence—carefully."

Madison nodded. "What are we—love detectives?"

They broke up into a fit of laughter.

The two BFFs had just finished having soup and salad with Madison's mom. Now they were sitting on the floor in the den. Mom believed they were going to watch a movie, but really they were trying to guess the true identity of Madison's admirer. Or, as Madison preferred to think of it, they were going to

find absolute proof that Hart was the one.

"So," Aimee said. "Let's make a list."

"A list of what?" Madison asked.

Aimee grinned. "A list of suspects," she said. "What else?"

"Ha-ha," Madison said.

"Now, as I see it," Aimee went on, "the prime suspects are Drew, Chet, Hart, Dan, Suresh, Lance, and Egg."

"What about Ben Buckley?" Madison asked.

Aimee shot her a look. "What about him?"

Madison smiled. "Aimee, why don't you just admit YOU like him."

"Whatever," Aimee said. "Can we please get on with this?"

"Why do you have Lance on that list?" Madison asked, crinkling her nose. "He's such a weirdo."

"True," Aimee admitted, tapping her lower lip. "We'll cross him off."

"And I hardly even know Suresh," Madison said. "I think he likes Lindsay Frost anyhow. She told me he might ask her to the dance."

"Really?" Aimee said. "Okay. Cross him off, too."

"Hey, you can cross off Egg, too," Madison said. "Have you forgotten that he likes Fiona?"

"Yeah, but Egg could be helping someone else by putting the things in your locker," Aimee explained. "So identifying him brings us closer to knowing who the real admirer is . . . right?"

Madison's eyes bulged. "I hadn't even thought of that," she said.

"And Egg knows more about you than any of those other guys," Aimee added.

Madison shrugged. "Okay. Put him on the list."

"All right," Aimee said. "Now we'll go one by one, and create a profile of each of the guys. Then we'll compare the evidence against the profile."

"The evidence?" Madison giggled. She grabbed a handful of popcorn. "I can type it up later, and even scan in the guys' photos."

"Then we can send the pages to the FBI," Aimee joked. "And see if they come up with anything."

Both girls laughed as Aimee typed "Walter Emilio Diaz" at the top of the page.

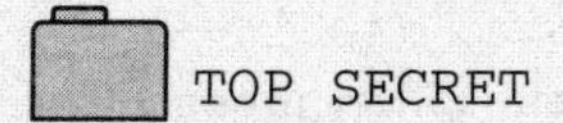

Walter Emilio Diaz

Alias: Egg

Score on Romance-O-Meter: probably a 5 out of 10, now that we've seen him offer to buy Fiona an ice-cream cone

Facts: Has known Madison since Miss Jeremiah's kindergarten class

Had a crush on Madison in first grade, therefore might be willing to help another boy who has a crush on Madison.

Knows where Madison lives, what she likes, etc.

Considers Madison his best gf—what does that really mean?

Profile summary: Possible accomplice

Madison giggled as she reread what Aimee had written. "It looks good on the screen. But the truth is that Egg probably wouldn't want to get involved in some love-match thing," she said.

"Yeah," Aimee agreed. "He knows we'd freak if we saw him putting something romantic in your locker."

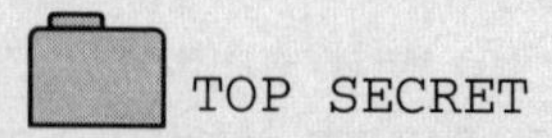

Andrew Maxwell

Alias: Drew

Score on Romance-O-Meter: unknown

Facts: Likes chocolate. (As in—chocolate roses??) Lives 15 minutes from Madison's house. It's unlikely he'd be able to drop off a card without Egg's help. HOWEVER, Egg is his best friend. Also good at computers—could send Orange Crush message secretly.

Profile summary: 20% chance he is our crusher

"Twenty percent?" Madison asked, reading what Aimee had typed. "What makes you say that?"

Aimee shrugged. "I think it's possible that he's the one, but there are some complications," she

explained. "I mean, he's too obvious. Everyone *knows* he likes you . . ."

"What do you mean, 'everyone knows'?" Madison asked.

Aimee made a clucking noise. "Maddie, c'mon. He always stares at you and sits near you. But I know you don't really like him that way, so . . ."

Madison couldn't believe what Aimee was saying. She always had the feeling that Drew was extra-nice to her, but she didn't know that *everyone* noticed.

"Look. Drew isn't exactly the King of Organization, so chances are that he wouldn't plan to send you secret messages. And Egg probably isn't helping him. Come to think of it, the whole idea that those two would be working together on some kind of romantic project seems kind of—" She searched for the word.

"Hilarious," Madison finished for her.

"Exactly." Aimee nodded, and the two girls went on to the next suspect.

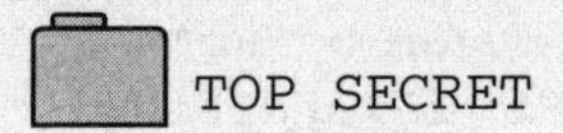
TOP SECRET

Daniel Ginsburg

Alias: Dan, Pork-O

Score on Romance-O-Meter: 3 or 4

Facts: Likes animals. LOVES food. Very, VERY funny. More like a brother to Madison than romantic.

Profile summary: 5% chance he is our crusher

"Why did you put five percent?" Madison asked Aimee.

"Well, Dan is a nice guy and all that, but I don't think it's him. I mean, he cares way more about french fries and chocolate-chip cookies than girls, right?" Aimee said. "What do you think?"

"He's nice," Madison said.

"Yeah, but he's not the dating type," Aimee said. "You know?"

Madison nodded and they moved along to the next suspect.

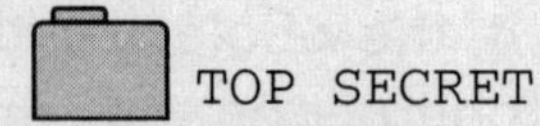
TOP SECRET

Chet Waters

Alias: None

Score on Romance-O-Meter: 0

Facts: He lives only a block away and could find out tons of info about Madison from Fiona. HOWEVER, Chet is way too goofy to think of sending secret admirer stuff to Madison. Besides, he'd never be able to keep it a secret from Fiona, and Fiona would never be able to keep it a secret from US!!

Profile summary: unlikely suspect

Aimee gave a funny little snort, and Madison looked over at her. "What?" she asked.

"I'm sorry," Aimee said with a giggle. "I was just picturing you and Chet on a double date with Fiona and Egg."

"Chet and Egg would start a food fight the minute Fiona and I went to the ladies' room," Madison said.

"That's just what I was thinking!" Aimee said, and she and Madison cracked up. "Okay, okay, we have to calm down, this is serious," Aimee said, leaning toward the computer.

Madison was about to start laughing again when she leaned over and saw what Aimee was typing. She pursed her lips and held her breath instead.

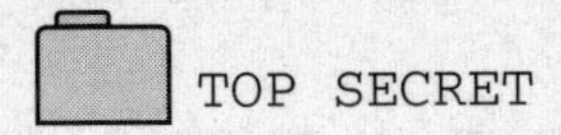

```
TOP SECRET
    Hart Jones
    Alias: None
    Score on Romance-O-Meter: 8
    Facts: Used to like Madison in second
 grade. Calls Madison by special name (even
 though it is dumb): The Finnster. Is good
 friends with Chet, and could find out
 information about Madison from both Fiona
 and/or Egg. Was in Madison's neighborhood
 at time of most recent card delivery.
    Profile summary: Prime suspect
```

"Do you really think he's the prime suspect?" Madison asked when she saw what Aimee had written.

Aimee bit her lip. "Well . . . he seems like the most likely person so far," she admitted. "But I'm not a hundred percent sure. I think he likes Ivy Daly a lot. He's always spending time with her and the drones, right?"

Madison peered at the screen, glancing at what they had written so far. "It could be any of these guys, or none of them," she said. "You didn't put that cute ninth grader on the list."

Aimee laughed. "Get real, Maddie. You're my best friend, but do you really think that he is going to ask you to the dance? He doesn't even know you."

Madison punched Aimee's shoulder lightly. "It could happen!"

Aimee smiled. "I should be getting home," she said. "It's late. I have to study."

"I guess we'll solve this mystery another time," Madison agreed, pushing herself to her feet. Her legs were stiff after sitting so long. "I'll walk with you. Phin needs to go out anyway."

Aimee said good-bye to Mom, who was reading a novel in the living room. "Be back in a few minutes," Madison told her, grabbing Phin's leash.

Phin kept sticking his nose way up in the air, sniffing like crazy. Madison wondered if he was trying to catch Peaches's scent.

"Hey," Aimee said as she walked up the steps to her house. "Should I get Blossom?"

Phin let out a big yawn.

"Nah, we'll see you tomorrow, Aim," Madison said.

"Okay," Aimee said. "Just don't forget about our Prime Suspect. I've got my eye on him now for sure."

Madison hurried away as Aimee said that. Luckily it was dark outside, so her friend couldn't see her turn four shades of pink. But one thing was true: if Aimee thought that Hart was the crusher, then it was DEFINITELY possible that he was the crusher. It was the law of averages, or something like that.

Madison smiled dreamily as she wandered down the street with Phin, imagining herself at the dance, wearing her new blue dress, holding Hart's arm, gloating in front of Ivy Daly and her obnoxious drones. . . .

Suddenly, Madison felt a tug on her leash. She turned and saw Phin was limping in the middle of the sidewalk.

"Come on, Phinnie," Madison urged. "It's cold out here and we need to get home." She tugged gently on the leash, but Phin didn't budge. He let out a yelp and lifted up his back paw.

"What's wrong? Is something wrong with your leg?" Madison asked, kneeling to look at Phin's paw. He was holding it off the ground.

"Oh, Phin," Madison said, her voice edged with worry. "What happened? Did you step on something?" Phin whimpered as she scooped him gingerly into her arms. "Don't worry," Madison whispered.

She jogged toward the house, careful not to jostle Phin too much. She wasn't really sure whether she was talking to Phin, or to herself.

"Mom!" Madison called out. "Come here! Phin's hurt!"

Mom ran into the front hall. "What's wrong?" she asked.

"His paw," Madison said, lifting his rear leg.

Phin was crying more now.

"We'd better get him to the clinic right away," Mom said, inspecting Phin's paw. "This looks really sore."

"But what is it?" Madison asked. She wrapped him in a soft blanket, grabbed her orange bag and followed Mom out the door. If I hadn't been so caught up in my daydreams about Hart, Madison thought, feeling guiltier than guilty, this never would have happened.

"Emergency!" Madison yelled as they walked through the doors of the Far Hills Animal Clinic. She had Phin cradled in her arms.

"What?" Eileen Ginsburg, Dan's mother and the nurse at the clinic, asked.

"I was walking Phinnie and . . ." Madison said breathlessly, "there's something wrong with his foot."

Phin let out a low whimper.

"Don't worry, pooch," Eileen said. "Everything will be F-I-N-E, fine."

Madison tried to smile at Eileen, who was wearing a T-shirt that read ONE COOL CAT with a photo of a tiger on the front. Dan's mom proudly wore something from her T-shirt collection to work every day. But it was hard to smile when Phinnie was in pain.

Eileen hurried to the rear of the clinic just as Mom walked in the door. She had been parking the car.

"Eileen is getting Dr. Wing," Madison explained. Mom nodded, and looked at Phin with a worried frown.

"Madison?" Eileen poked her head through the door that led to the back. "Come back to exam room two. Dr. Wing is ready for you."

"Hi, Dr. Wing," Madison said as she entered the room. She gently put Phin on the table. Madison knew Dr. Wing pretty well for two reasons. He was married to Madison's favorite computer teacher, Mrs. Wing. He also had been the one to suggest that Madison volunteer at the clinic.

"This is my mom," Madison said.

Mom extended her hand. "Frannie Finn," she said. "Sorry to meet under these circumstances. I've heard so much about this place."

"And how's our patient?" Dr. Wing asked as he looked at Phin. "Phineas, do you have a paw problem?"

"You remember his name?" Madison said, impressed.

"Ah, I see what we have here," Dr. Wing said as he examined Phin's paw. "It looks as though a few small stones have gotten wedged between his nails and the pads of his feet. It's infected."

"He stepped on something?" Madison asked.

"Yes, a few days ago, most likely," Dr. Wing said, pulling a pair of tweezers and some other instruments out of a drawer. Madison breathed a sigh of relief that her daydreaming hadn't been the cause of Phin's injury.

He instructed Madison and Mom to hold the dog's head as still as possible. Eileen controlled Phin's torso and legs.

"Now, Phineas, this is only going to hurt for a second." Phin yelped loudly as Dr. Wing pulled each pebble out of his paw. Then Phin tried to chew at his foot.

"No, no, no," Dr. Wing said.

Eileen gently moved Phin's head back away from the paw, as the doctor quickly smeared some ointment on Phin's foot and wrapped it with a bandage. Of course, Phin sniffed at that, too.

"Rooooowwwwwroooo!" he wailed.

"Come back in ten days, and we'll take this off," Dr. Wing said. "Just try to keep this area as clean as possible. Eileen will give you more bandages. Change the bandage each day or whenever he bites off the one he's wearing. He will chew at it."

"Oh, thank you, Dr. Wing," Madison said as she

scooped Phin up into her arms. She was careful not to squash the wounded paw.

Dr. Wing grinned. "No problem, Madison. All in a day's work."

Mom shook Dr. Wing's hand, then they went out front to pay.

Dan was waiting there. "Is everything okay?" he asked, casting a worried look toward Phin.

Madison nodded. "Dr. Wing says he'll be better in no time," she said.

"Whew! That's good news," Dan said with a smile. "Isn't Dr. Wing the best?"

Madison agreed. "I am so glad there's nothing seriously wrong. I was worried."

Dan patted Phin on the head. Phin licked Dan's hand.

"Gee, he likes you," Madison said. "He doesn't usually give out kisses like that."

"Oh, yeah?" Dan asked, bouncing on his toes. Madison thought that he seemed a little nervous with his mom sitting so close by.

"Hey, is that llama still here?" Madison asked.

"Discharged yesterday," Dan said. "Too bad you missed her."

"Hey, Dan, can I ask you something?" Madison asked.

"Sure thing," Dan joked. "What do you want—my autograph?"

"Very funny," Madison said, chuckling. "No. I

wanted to know if you are going to the Heart to Heart dance. Are you?"

Dan shrugged again. "Yeah, I think I'm going," he said. "Why . . . are you asking me or something?"

Madison smiled. "Um . . . not exactly," she said.

"Um . . . I was just kidding," Dan said.

"But I *am* going to the dance," Madison said. "Even with no date."

Standing there, Madison was reminded of Hart, or at least of the fact that Dan was a good friend of Hart. Maybe *Dan* had a clue about Madison's secret admirer. Maybe he could help uncover the truth?

"Do you know anyone *else* who's going?" she asked, hoping for more clues. "Or someone who wants to go with someone, but is maybe too shy or . . ." Madison cut herself off. "I shouldn't be asking you this. Sorry."

"I haven't really asked around," Dan said. "I can if you want."

"No, that's okay," Madison nodded, trying to hide her disappointment. "I didn't mean to say all that. I feel pretty stupid."

Madison tried to act cool, but she was afraid she'd just revealed too much to Dan. What if he went back to Hart and said something?

Mom came up behind her and tapped Madison on the shoulder. "We should get going."

"Don't forget your bag, Madison," Eileen said,

holding up Madison's orange book bag. She'd left it inside the examination room.

"Thanks," Madison told Eileen as she took the bag. "See you at school, Dan?" Madison added.

"Yeah," Dan said with a smile. "See you around."

Dan stood at the large glass window to wave good-bye. Madison carried Phin outside and climbed into the car with the dog in her lap. She waved back.

"That boy seems nice," Mom said as she started the engine.

"Yeah, he is," Madison said as she stroked Phin's fur.

Phin nuzzled deeper into Madison's lap. Her dog was still the number-one boy in her life.

Chapter 8

The sign on Mr. Gibbons's classroom door read OUTLINES DUE TODAY. Madison couldn't believe it was already the week the paper was due. She and Fiona had barely coordinated their ideas.

Madison had tried to call Fiona the night before to run the John and Abigail Adams idea past her, but Chet had been hogging the phone—as usual. So she typed up what she had and shared it with Fiona before class. She had to hurry *and* she had to keep her fingers crossed that the idea would work out.

Just as the first class bell rang, Madison remembered that she'd left her English notebook in her locker, so she hustled back to get it. Her books were wedged in there so tightly that she had to give the

notebook a yank before it moved. And when it finally did pop free, that sent half of her books tumbling to the floor in a paper avalanche.

As Madison leaned over to pick up her dropped social studies textbook, a piece of paper flew out of it. She flipped it over, and saw that FOR MADISON was printed neatly on one side.

But how had it gotten inside her social studies book?

I am not a poet
And I truly know it,
But I think you're really cool,
So I thought I'd show it!
(I hope this goofy rhyme of mine
Doesn't totally blow it!)

signed, Your Secret Admirer

Madison laughed out loud. She folded the note carefully and stuck it into her English notebook so she could show it to Fiona and Aimee later. Unfortunately, this piece of evidence didn't really help. For one thing, it was a poem and none of the boys they knew wrote poems. But on the other hand, all of the boys they knew were pretty funny. Maybe one of them *did* write this.

Madison's heart was betting on Hart.

Sometimes I carry my social studies book with me

to science class, Madison thought. So Hart could have snuck the note inside it then. And who knows how long that note has even been there?

Madison smiled to herself, picturing how Hart thought up the little rhyme and put the poem into her book.

"Hey, Finnster!" Hart's voice seemed loud and clear.

He was standing right there beside Madison, as if she'd willed him there.

Is he going to say something about the note? Is he going to admit that he's my secret admirer? Before she could realize what she was doing, Madison turned on her heel and ran in the opposite direction.

"Finnster, wait up!" Hart called, but Madison wouldn't wait. Her feet wouldn't let her.

And as if things weren't already bad enough, Madison turned a corner and smacked straight into Ivy. Madison's books and pink flyers flew everywhere.

"Ow," Ivy said, rubbing her shoulder. "Why don't you watch where you're going?"

"Sorry," Madison said quickly as she bent toward her books.

Ivy got up and walked away without saying anything.

Madison shrugged, and reached for her English book, but she saw that a hand was already holding it out to her. She caught her breath as she looked up and saw—

"Drew!" Madison said, head spinning with relief. "Oh, it's just you."

"*Just* me?" Drew joked.

Madison laughed as she took the book from him and stood up. "No—sorry. I meant—it's you! Great!"

Drew smiled. "That's more like it," he said. Then cleared his throat and asked, "You're headed to English, right? Mind if I walk with you?"

"Okay," Madison said.

Drew smiled and his whole face lit up. "Cool," he said.

They fell into step toward Mr. Gibbons's class, but Drew didn't say anything for a little while, which made Madison a little uncomfortable. Usually, Drew was a talkative guy. In no time, they were standing in front of Mr. Gibbons's classroom.

"Well, here's where I get off," Madison said.

"Wait a sec—" Drew said, his voice getting quiet. "Maddie, there's something I've been meaning to ask you."

"Ask me?" Madison said slowly, her voice barely above a whisper. "Is everything all right?"

"Oh—yeah," Drew said. He took Madison's elbow and gently pulled her to the side, so that other kids could get into the room. He looked at her a moment, and for the first time, Madison noticed that there were flecks of gold in his brown hair. Even though Drew wore it in a spiky hairdo, which made

it look different, Madison realized that Drew's hair was actually just like Hart's.

Drew looked at the floor, and traced a crack in the stone with the toe of his shoe. "You know, Fiona and Egg are going to the dance together."

"I know. Isn't it weird?" Madison said.

"Yeah, well," Drew went on, looking back at his shoes, "I was thinking that it could be fun if we went together, too. Like, as a double date."

He paused, then looked up at her expectantly.

Madison felt so dumb. She remembered what Aimee had said the day before about him liking her.

How could she not have seen this coming?

"Gee," Madison said, taking a long time to respond. She was confused. Drew wanted *her* to be his date? *Drew* was asking her to the dance? Did this mean Drew was Orange Crush?

"I don't think I can go," Madison said. "No, I definitely can't."

"No?" Drew said.

Madison stood there a moment, unable to believe that she had just turned him down—just like that.

Drew blinked a few times, like someone had just punched him in the stomach. He jammed his fists into his pockets. "So," he said, nodding. "You're not going to the dance?"

"Not exactly," Madison said.

"Oh, I get it," Drew said. "You're just not going with me."

"I'm sorry," Madison said in a rush. "It's just that I already promised someone else—"

Madison felt her face grow hot at the lie. What was wrong with her? Why did she keep saying things that weren't true?

Drew looked away for a minute, and when he glanced back his eyes looked sad, like the way Phinnie's did when he wanted to go out.

"I'm really, really, REALLY sorry," Madison said.

"I understand," Drew said.

Madison sighed. She felt as though he really *did* understand, which made her feel even worse. She opened her mouth to apologize again, but the bell rang, drowning out both of their voices momentarily.

"I'd better get to class," Drew said. He turned and jogged away.

I should run after him, Madison thought. I should tell him that I made a mistake, and that I WILL go to the dance with him.

But Madison's feet didn't move an inch. She couldn't move—she was too confused. Had Drew been lurking near her locker to see what she would do when she got his note? When he saw Madison giggling at the rhyme, had Drew decided to ask her to the dance? Aimee gave Drew a twenty-percent chance of being her admirer. So it was probably true.

Egg must have been helping him all along.

"Are you planning to join us sometime today, Ms. Finn?" Mr. Gibbons asked from the doorway.

Madison didn't reply. She walked inside silently, sat at a desk, and took out her notebook, staring at the blank page for a long time.

If Drew was Orange Crush, it meant Hart *wasn't*.

All the horoscopes in the world couldn't change that one.

By the time Madison sat down at her computer that night with Phin curled comfortably at her feet, some of the Drew guilt was fading. Now all Madison wanted to do was to write to Bigwheels and tell her everything that had happened. Bigwheels was one person who would understand why Madison had done what she did to Drew. She knew how Madison felt about Hart.

But an e-mail to Bigwheels would have to wait. Madison had a ton of mail to read through first.

She scrolled through the messages, looking for another one from her secret admirer.

FROM	SUBJECT
✉ JeffFinn	Dinner
✉ Far Hills Animal Clinic	Flower power
✉ Balletgrl	Where were U?
✉ Eggaway	<no subject>
✉ Wetwinz	The Dance

Madison sighed. Of course there aren't any messages from your admirer, she told herself. Your admirer is Drew. And why would he send you a message after you totally torpedoed him today?

The first message was from Dad, asking if she wanted to have dinner at Stephanie's the following night—to make up for the getting sick episode a week earlier at Tamales. Madison sent back a quick note saying that she'd love to see them. Then she clicked on the next message.

She expected it to be from Dr. Wing about Phin, but instead it was from Dan.

```
From: Far Hills Animal Clinic
To: MadFinn
Subject: Flower Power
Date: Tues 11 Feb 3:02 PM
```

```
Hey, there? How's the pup? I hope
Phin is okay and that he is running
around on his fixed-up foot.
Are you getting excited about the
Heart to Heart dance? I've already
sold more than 20 carnations. RU
selling any? I think it's a cool
fundraiser, even if Ivy Daly is in
charge of it. :-P

By the way, are either of yr
parents going to chaperone the
dance? My mom is going to be there.
```

I can't decide if that's a good thing or a bad thing.

Dan

Madison shot back a quick reply.

From: MadFinn
To: Far Hills Animal Clinic
Subject: Re: Flower Power
Date: Tues 11 Feb 5:13 PM

Hi, Dan!
Phin is fine. He is curled up by my feet, sleeping away. His foot doesn't seem to bother him one bit.

Wow! I can't believe you've already sold 20 flowers! Who are you selling them to—the puppies and kittens at the clinic? I bet that llama would love some flowers as a nice snack! LOL.

I haven't asked my mom to be a chaperone, but maybe I will. I know they're still looking for volunteers. And if yr. mom is anything like my mom, I'm sure she won't make a big deal about it.

See ya,

Maddie

Madison opened Aimee's e-mail next.

From: Balletgrl
To: MadFinn
Subject: Where were U?
Date: Tues 11 Feb 3:57 PM

Hi! I looked all over for U after school, but you were nowhere to be found! N-e-way, I have some info for our profiles, and FYA. Hart was totally hanging out by yr locker after fifth period. He looked like he wanted to talk to U. I still say he is our PRIME SUSPECT!!

Let me know if you have any more info.

SYS.

Aimee

Madison read Aimee's e-mail three times before she believed it. Hart was hanging by her locker before fifth? Maybe he was her secret admirer, after all?

She grinned as she opened the next e-mail, which was from Egg.

From: Eggaway
To: MadFinn
Subject: no subject
Date: Tues 11 Feb 3:29 PM

I can't blieve you totally hurt Drew's feeling's like that. dont you know how hard it was for him to ask you to the dance? dont you get it? Drew is a relly good guy, Maddie. I don't know what your problem is. You can't just do that to people.

Egg

PS: So ur going to the dance with someone else? IYD. I don't believe it. And Drew doesnt, either.

Madison swallowed hard. Great. Now Egg was mad at her. And the worst part was—he was right. Madison hit REPLY right away.

From: MadFinn
To: Eggaway
Subject: Re: no subject
Date: Tues 11 Feb 4:58 PM

I'm so sorry, Egg. I know I hurt

Drew's feelings and I feel really badly about it. I'll send an e-mail to Drew so that he knows how sorry I am. You're right, he really is a good guy. Please don't be mad.

Madison

Maybe this e-mail will cheer me up, Madison thought as she clicked on the final e-mail, a note from Fiona.

From: Wetwinz
To: MadFinn
Subject: The Dance
Date: Tues 11 Feb 3:17 PM

Maddie,

Egg just told me that Drew asked you to the dance and you said no??? Egg is pretty mad about it, so don't be surprised if he sends you an e-mail, too. I know that you must have had a good reason for doing what you did, but you should know that you really hurt Drew's feelings. Egg told me Drew's been planning to ask you for a whole week.

RU really going with someone else?

```
I don't know what to think, because
I think you would have told me if
someone had asked U to the dance.
But I also know that it isn't like
you to tell a lie, so I'm waiting
to hear.

WBL, Fiona
```

Madison bit her lip.

Did everyone in the entire universe know about what had happened with Drew? It seemed that way. Was there anything that she could say in an e-mail that would make things better?

"Honey bear?" Mom asked from the doorway just as Madison clicked SEND. "I was thinking I might go get a movie for us to watch tonight. Want to come help me pick it out?"

"Sure," Madison said.

But she didn't move.

"Everything okay?" Mom asked.

Madison shrugged. "I don't know," she said. "There's this school dance coming up . . ." Madison started. "Would you mind chaperoning it? It's on Friday."

"Love to," Mom said.

Madison pulled a sheet out of her backpack that Ivy had handed out in homeroom, and Mom signed it on the back. "Sounds like fun."

Madison nodded. "I guess," she said.

"You don't sound very enthusiastic," Mom said.

Madison shook her head. "It's just—I don't know what to do. I don't have a date."

Mom's eyebrows went up. "No boys asked you? I'm surprised."

"Well . . ." Madison hedged. She wasn't sure that she wanted to tell her mom everything. But then Madison thought about the e-mails. Everyone else in the whole world knew what had happened, so why shouldn't Mom?

"Actually, Mom, Drew asked me."

Mom smiled. "But . . . you said no," she said gently.

Madison nodded. "How did you know?"

Mom didn't say anything for a minute. "Mother's intuition."

"I'm impressed, Mom," she said.

"Why didn't you say yes, Maddie?" she asked finally. "You were looking for a date. Why not Drew?"

"I don't know!" Madison wailed, even though that wasn't exactly the truth. "I just . . . I just don't feel ready for a real date right now, you know? Well, not with him, anyhow."

"Okay." Mom folded her arms across her chest and leaned against the doorframe. "You know, I think you'll have fun no matter what—whether you're just with your friends, or with Drew."

"Not after today," Madison said.

"Well, I think Drew is probably more embarrassed than anything. And who knows? He may ask you out again."

"Mom, you don't understand. I really hurt his feelings," Madison admitted.

"Everybody gets their feelings hurt, sometimes," Mom said gently. "Even you. Even Drew."

"I guess," Madison said. "Can we not talk about this anymore?"

"Okay," Mom said, pausing. "Why don't you come down when you're ready? I'll be in the kitchen."

"Thanks, Mom."

Madison was barefoot, so she had to pull on her shoes and socks before they went to the video store. She kept wondering if rejecting Drew had been a big mistake.

But a little voice in her head whispered, *Don't forget! Hart is the Prime Suspect.*

There was still a chance that *he* might ask her to the dance, right?

If that happened, there was no way Madison would pass up going with him. Not even if it meant hurting a few more feelings along the way.

Chapter 9

"Hey, Maddie, pass me the red paint?" Aimee asked as she dipped her paintbrush into a jelly jar, staining the clear water inside a brilliant blue.

Madison reached for the large tub of "Some Kind of Scarlet" paint and slid it over to her best friend. She and Aimee were on their knees in the art studio, earning extra credit by painting a giant poster for the dance that read YOU GOTTA HAVE HEART . . . 2 HEART!

Aimee dotted little hearts and stars around the border while Madison filled in the letters. Several other kids on the other side of the studio worked on a different banner. Madison was surprised that so few people were trying for the extra credit. But

it was fun. Their teacher had only just posted the assignment in class this morning. Madison guessed that maybe most kids had other plans.

"Is Fiona coming up here to paint?" Madison asked Aimee, trying to sound casual as she filled in an H with red.

"Yeah," Aimee said, frowning at the lopsided heart she had just painted. "I saw her talking to Egg at his locker, though, so she could be a while."

Madison nodded. After receiving Fiona's crabby e-mail, Madison had spoken in person with her the night before. Madison tried to explain why she had turned Drew down. Fiona told her that she understood why Madison had said no, but that she shouldn't have lied to Drew about having another date. But still, her BFF promised to talk to Egg.

"I hope she convinces Egg that I'm not a horrible ogre," Madison said with a sigh.

Aimee smiled at Madison. "You're *not* a bad person," she reassured her.

She was staying sympathetic through the whole ordeal. "Besides, Egg never stays mad about things for long."

"Thanks for being such a good friend," Madison said.

"Yeah, well . . ." Aimee's face broke into a wide grin, and her brown eyes danced. "Do you want to know a secret?" she asked.

"What is it?" Madison asked eagerly.

"Ben Buckley asked me to the dance right after fourth period," Aimee said.

Madison's eyes popped. "No way!" she shrieked.

When a few kids turned around and stared, Madison pretended to be fascinated with the letter *E* she was painting. She bent over it and hid her face with her hair. "So—what did you say?" Madison asked.

"I said I'd think about it," Aimee said.

Madison's eyebrows flew up. "Think about it? Really?" she asked.

"At least for a few hours," Aimee shrugged. "After all, Ben is cute. And he asked me so nicely that I didn't know how to say no."

Madison laughed. "Now YOU can double-date with Fiona and Egg," she said.

Aimee laughed. "That's what I was thinking," she said.

Madison laughed a little, too, but inside she felt a pang. What was she talking about? Now *all* of her best friends had dates? Aimee had Ben, Fiona and Egg had each other, and Madison had—nobody?

She frowned as she dipped her brush into the red paint. Fiona arrived a few moments later.

"Hey, look at this!" Fiona wailed. She hurried into the art studio waving a hot-pink flyer.

"More flyers?" Madison asked. "Is Ivy on a mission to use up all of the hot-pink paper in the United States, or something?"

"It's the rules for the dance," Fiona explained.

"You won't believe it—there are about a thousand of them."

Aimee took the flyer from Fiona's hand and read. "Oh, yeah. Dean warned me about this," she said. "The year he was in eighth grade, the dance got really out of hand. It was Mr. Bernard's first year as principal, and you know how he can be. He went way overboard making up rules."

"Do we really have to do all of this?" Madison said, looking at the list. The Heart to Heart dance was looking like less fun by the minute.

"Most of the rules are no biggie," Fiona said. "They're handing the list to all students tomorrow morning, in homeroom."

Madison, Aimee, and Fiona crouched on the art studio floor and read the rules together. There were ten in all, and at the bottom of the page was a space for the student to sign, indicating that they agreed to abide by everything.

1. Dance open only to Far Hills Junior High students.

"Like, who else would want to come?" Aimee asked. "Students from Far Hills University?"

2. To attend the dance, students must have a school dance ticket listing phone number where parents can be reached.

"Oh, we have to buy our tickets," Fiona said. "Don't forget!"

"Right," Madison agreed.

3. Students may not leave the dance area to go elsewhere, including school classrooms.

"Why would we want to go to one of the classrooms?" Madison asked. "In case we want to brush up on some algebra on a Friday night?"

Aimee giggled. "No—to go make out!"

Madison turned pink. She couldn't believe she hadn't figured that one out.

4. Parents must pick up students promptly at 9:30 P.M., or students will lose their privileges to attend the next dance.

"That's not fair," Madison said. "If the parents are late, they should take away the parents' privileges!"

"Keep dreaming," Fiona told her.

5. Screaming, yelling, running, and game playing are NOT permitted.

"At least they allow *dancing*," Aimee said.

6. A respectable dance position is expected of all dancing couples.

The friends were silent for a moment, then burst out laughing.

"I can't believe they wrote that!" Madison cried.

Aimee whooped. "You'd better warn Egg!" she said to Fiona.

7. Students are not permitted to remove their shoes during the dance.

"The gym smells bad enough as it is," Madison added in an official-sounding voice.

"We will not be held responsible for students contracting foot fungus from the disgusting gym floor," Fiona put in.

8. Students are expected to keep the hallways and dance areas free and clear of all wrappers and cups. Keep snacks in the snack zone.

"The snack zone?" Madison asked. "What's that?"

"It sounds like a made-for-TV movie," Aimee suggested.

"When good snacks go bad," Fiona added.

The girls laughed.

9. Students must be in attendance for the full school day on the day of the dance.

"I overheard Ivy say that she was going to blow off her last class to go home and get dressed," Madison said.

"Let's hope she does it," Aimee said. "Then maybe she'll get busted."

As if I could ever get that lucky, Madison thought. Having Ivy out of the whole dance equation would make life much mellower.

```
10. Proper clothing is required.
    Dances are a dress-up event.
    Denim jeans, baggy pants,
    tight pants, halter tops, and
    thick-soled or platform shoes are
    not permitted. Clothing should be
    free of all rips, tears, and
    frayed material.
```

"What do they have against thick-soled shoes?" Madison asked.

"Whatever," Fiona said. "I'm wearing ballet flats, so I don't really care."

"Why would anyone wear torn clothing to a dance?" Aimee asked.

"No clue," Fiona said. "Although Egg is going to be mad that he can't go in his jeans. Personally, I don't know what he's griping about. I love to get dressed up."

"Me, too," Madison agreed.

"I just hope they play some good dance music,"

Fiona said. "The DJ at my old school was always so lame. Half of the songs he played were country and western."

"That definitely won't be happening this time," Aimee assured her. "The DJ they hired plays mostly hip-hop and pop, with a little rock thrown in."

"We'll see if I can manage to drag Egg onto the dance floor," Fiona said.

"Good luck," Aimee said with a smile. "Egg hates dancing."

"All guys claim they hate dancing," Madison said.

"I've seen Ben dancing at parties sometimes," Aimee said. Fiona grinned at her and she turned pink. "What?"

"Does this mean that you're going to say yes to Ben?" Fiona asked.

Aimee shrugged, then giggled. "I think so," she said.

Madison dipped her paintbrush in the water, turning the blue to purple. "We should start cleaning up," she said quickly.

"Maddie, why don't you reconsider going with Drew?" Fiona asked as she screwed the lid back on the tub of red paint. "I mean, it doesn't have to be any big deal. . . ."

"Yeah, Maddie," Aimee agreed. "Then we can be on a *triple* date!"

Madison shrugged and smiled at her friends. "Thanks. But I just don't think . . ." Her voice trailed

off. The truth was, she had no idea what she thought. Maybe she was crazy to say no to Drew. But somehow, she just didn't feel right saying yes.

"Okay, I have an idea," Aimee said. "Why don't Fiona and I tell Egg and Ben that we'll meet them at the dance? That way, the three of us can show up together, and you won't have to feel like you're coming by yourself. And I promise I won't ask Drew to come. That would be weird."

Madison grinned at her friend. Sometimes, it was as though Aimee could read her mind. "That sounds great!" Madison said.

"Good idea," Fiona said. "And we can meet at Madison's house and do our hair together and stuff."

"Yes!" Aimee agreed.

As she walked out the front door to the school with her two best friends, Madison felt as though a heavy weight had been lifted from her chest.

So what if she didn't have a date for the dance?

She was going with her friends—and she was going to have a good time.

Dad picked Madison up a little early that night so they could run an errand before going to Stephanie's house for dinner. The mall was practically empty as the two of them walked through Far Hill Shoppes. Madison didn't see too many familiar faces.

As they walked past a store called Over Hair,

something glittery caught Madison's eye. She turned to see a display of all sorts of clips, barrettes, and other accessories. In the center of the window was a display of small tiaras. One of them was set with blue stones. Madison stopped to take a closer look. Poison Ivy had worn one to the *last* school dance, and even though Madison wasn't wild about her personality, she had to admit that the enemy had fashion sense.

"What's that?" Dad asked.

"Oh—just that little tiara," Madison admitted.

"A tiara?" Dad asked. "Something you like?"

"For the dance, maybe," Madison explained. "The blue one would go with my new dress."

"So let's get it," Dad said.

"Oh!" Madison said, surprised by her dad's offer. "Are you sure?"

"It would look beautiful on you," Dad said with a grin. "As they say, diamonds are a girl's best friend—and fake sapphires are her other best friends."

Madison beamed.

"But we'd better be quick. I don't want to be late getting to Stephanie's. She's planning a feast."

Dad bought the tiara and the woman wrapped it in paper and put it into a tiny shopping bag, which she handed to Madison. Just thinking about wearing it at the dance made Madison feel very glamorous. She swung the bag by her side as she followed Dad through the mall.

"I have one more pit stop," Dad said, stopping in

front of a store. Madison looked up. She saw the JEWEL OF THE NILE sign.

Help! Madison thought to herself. This was the store that Madison had seen her dad in the other day. Were they here to pick up the engagement ring? Bigwheels had advised Madison to ask Dad about the ring, but when the moment of truth came . . . she couldn't ask much of anything.

"Mr. Finn, so good to see you," the store manager said when he saw Dad. "You'll be happy to hear that the engraving is finished." The clerk's face was perfectly round like a doughnut, and his smooth skin shone as he smiled.

"Thanks, Abe," Dad said, "I can't wait to see how it came out."

The manager pulled out a small black box—*the* small black box—and handed it to Dad. Madison hovered in the doorway. She couldn't bring herself to set foot in the store.

She watched as Dad pulled out his wallet and handed the manager a silver credit card.

"Do you want to see the best Valentine's Day gift ever?" Dad asked, walking over to Madison.

Weakly, Madison shook her head no, but her father wasn't paying attention. He undid the latch on the box.

Madison opened her mouth to speak, but she couldn't get the words out. All she wanted to say was no. No—she didn't want to see an engagement

ring. No—she didn't want to think about her father asking Stephanie to marry him.

No, no, no.

Madison's mind reeled as her father pulled open the box to reveal what was inside.

"Earrings?" Madison asked, staring at the silver ovals.

"Cuff links," her dad corrected. "It's a gift for one of my clients—a terrific guy. He's retiring on Valentine's Day. Look, I had them engraved." He pulled out one of the cuff links and turned it over so that Madison could see the back.

"Cuff links?" Madison choked on the words. She was so relieved, her eyes could hardly focus on the letters. She just started to giggle so hard that her shoulders shook.

"What's so funny?" Dad asked. The corners of his mouth were curved into a smile, eager to share the joke.

Madison thought about telling him what she thought would be in the box, but rejected the idea. The last thing she wanted to do was put ideas into his head.

"Nothing's funny," Madison said, taking deep breaths to stop her laughter. "I just remembered something that Egg said, that's all."

Dad shrugged and signed the credit card receipt.

Madison smiled all the way back to the car.

Chapter 10

"Greetings!" Stephanie said as she pulled open the door to her condo. "Come on in."

A delicious smell wafted past Madison's nose as she stepped into the apartment. It was sweet like apples and spicy like cinnamon.

Dad leaned over to give Stephanie a quick kiss on the cheek as Madison looked around. She had never been to Stephanie's apartment before. All of her furniture was sleek, dark wood and leather, and it was very clean and tidy. There were no shoes or magazines lying anywhere.

"Mmmmm," Madison said, as she followed Stephanie into the kitchen. "What are we having?"

"Moroccan stew," Stephanie said, taking the lid

off of a pot and stirring the contents with a wooden spoon. "I hope you like tangy food."

"Sounds great," Madison said warmly. She put her orange backpack on the floor. "Can I help with something?"

"You can chop up some veggies for a salad," Stephanie said. "They're in the fridge."

"I can definitely handle that." Madison walked over to the enormous steel refrigerator and pulled out some yellow bell peppers, carrots, and cucumbers. Even the inside of Stephanie's fridge was clean, and all of her leftovers were in tidy Tupperware boxes. "Do you like to cook?" Madison asked. For some reason, the idea surprised her. Maybe because she always saw Stephanie in restaurants, never bustling around a kitchen in a dark green apron, as she was doing now.

"I love it," Stephanie said as she wrapped some crusty bread in aluminum foil and placed it in the oven to warm. Stephanie had the nicest stove that Madison had ever seen. It was steel too, like the refrigerator, and the gas flames licked the bottom of a large gray pot with steel handles. "Sometimes, if I've had a frustrating day at work, I just come home and cook up a storm."

Dad was a good cook, too. He always said that some people relaxed with exercise, but he preferred to relax with good food.

Madison pulled a knife with a black handle from

the wooden block on the countertop and began chopping the bell peppers on a white cutting board. Since her mom was a vegetarian, Madison had plenty of experience cutting up vegetables.

Through the kitchen door, Madison could see her dad lighting candles on the dining room table. Then he walked into the kitchen with a lit candle and placed it on the countertop. "A little ambience," Dad said, dimming the overhead lights.

"How elegant," Stephanie said. She opened a cupboard and pulled out two more candlesticks. "Let's have a few more."

Dad lit the candles and placed them around the kitchen. They lit the room with a warm yellow glow. Putting down her knife, Madison bent down to her bag and pulled out her new blue tiara.

"As long as we're being elegant . . ." Madison said, putting on the tiara.

"Now I wish I had a tuxedo," Dad said. "Since I'm surrounded by you two gorgeous girls." He came up behind Stephanie and gave her a hug. Stephanie looked up at him and kissed him on the cheek.

"Oh, Dad," Madison said. But unlike the night at Tamales, she didn't feel so sick over it. Valentine's Day was coming closer. It was okay for Dad and Stephanie to be acting all lovey-dovey tonight.

"Photo op!" Dad said, pulling his digital camera out of a small black bag.

First, he took a picture of Stephanie tasting the stew.

Then he turned to Madison, who smiled as she cut a carrot into small round slices. He showed Madison the picture of herself on the camera's tiny monitor.

The warm candlelight made her skin glow pink, and the tiny blue tiara sparkled softly in her hair. Maybe she could look pretty for the dance after all? Maybe she could win Hart's heart with her new blue tiara?

"I'll e-mail you a copy of this for Mom," Dad said.

"That would be great," Madison said. "Actually, Dad, could I borrow your camera for the dance?" she asked.

Dad shrugged. "I don't see why not."

"Mrs. Wing is looking for someone to be the event photographer. She'd like to have some pictures of the dance on the school Web site," Madison explained.

"That sounds like a great idea," Stephanie said.

"It's all yours," Dad said. "I can even help you post the photos on the site after the dance." He leaned over and showed Madison how the functions worked and which buttons to press. Madison practiced her skills by taking a photo of Dad and Stephanie. They looked so happy together.

"It looks like we're about ready," Stephanie said, pulling together some final ingredients. She got out

three bowls, and spooned some fluffy brown stuff into the bottom of each.

"What's that?" Madison asked.

"Couscous," Stephanie said. "It goes with the stew." Stephanie ladled some stew on top of the couscous as Dad pulled the bread out of the oven and put it into a basket. Madison put the finishing touches on her salad, spreading the long strips of bell pepper into a circle. Stephanie and Dad raved about the salad.

"This is delicious," Madison said, taking a bite of the thick spicy stew. It made her whole body warm.

"Stephanie is a great cook," Dad said, reaching for Stephanie's hand.

Stephanie blushed.

"I have a Valentine's Day surprise for you," Dad said as Madison took another bite of stew.

Madison looked up, and was surprised to see that Dad was talking to her, not to Stephanie. "What is it?" she asked eagerly.

"If I tell you, it won't be a surprise," Dad said. He pulled a large box out from beneath the table, and put it down beside Madison's plate. "Happy Valentine's Day," Dad said.

Madison stood up and tore the paper off the box. She loved getting presents, but surprise presents were the best. She lifted the cardboard box lid and pulled out white tissue paper to reveal a large stuffed animal.

"A pug!" Madison squealed. She pulled it out of

the box and gave it a big hug right away. "It's just like Phin!" she said. "I love it!"

"Read the tag," Dad said.

Madison felt around the dog's neck. I WOOF U, the metal tag read. The letters blurred as tears grew in Madison's eyes. "Thanks, Dad," she whispered. "I've had so much fun tonight!"

"Me, too," Stephanie added.

As Dad drove her home, Madison sat quietly, hugging the stuffed pug on her lap. Madison was happy that Dad had found someone like Stephanie. And she was happier than happy that there was no engagement ring . . . *yet*.

"Here we are! Door-to-door service," Dad said as he pulled up in front of Madison's house.

"Good night, Dad," Madison said, leaning over to give him a kiss.

"Madison," Dad said, taking Madison's hand and lacing his fingers through hers. "I hope you have a good time at the school dance. I hope that boy you like does ask you to go with him."

"Thanks, Dad," Madison said.

Dad kissed her hand and reached out to touch her tiara, as if she were a fairy princess. "You're growing up," he said.

"Yes, I am," Madison said.

"Well—no matter how grown up you get, will you always be my valentine?" Dad asked.

"Of course," Madison promised, and she meant it. She gave her dad another kiss. "Good night," she said, racing up the porch steps and inside the house. Dad waited for her to get in.

Madison peeked into her mom's office before heading to her room. Her mom was typing furiously, frowning at her computer monitor. "Mom?" Madison said softly.

"Madison!" Mom's face broke into a smile. "Hi, honey bear. I didn't hear you come in."

"Are you going to be up late?" Madison asked.

"Probably," Mom admitted. "Are you going to bed?"

"Not yet," Madison said. "I've got some homework . . . and some e-mails to write," she added, thinking about Bigwheels.

"I'll be up in an hour," Mom said.

"Okay," Madison said, promising not to stay up too late. Then she shut her mom's office door gently and padded upstairs to her room. Phin was already fast asleep on her bed as Madison walked into her room. His bandaged leg stuck out at a funny angle. She put the stuffed pug on her pillow and smiled, wondering what Phin would think of it when he woke up.

Madison booted up her computer. She owed Bigwheels an e-mail. But to Madison's surprise. Bigwheels had already sent her a second message. She clicked on the e-mail.

From: Bigwheels
To: MadFinn
Subject: Luv is all U Need!
Date: Wed 12 Feb 8:38 PM

So today, when I went to my locker, there was a note inside for me. It was from Reggie, and it was a poem—he wrote it for me! It said "Roses are red, violets are blue, I wrote this poem, just for YOU!" I just can't believe that I actually have a boyfriend who is romantic! Am I lucky, or what?

I'm so excited for the dance!! I'm going to wear my red velvet dress because Reggie said that my red sweater is his favorite. He loves the color red. Of course, I think Reggie looks way cute in everything he wears, so I told him that I wanted him to wear—

Ugh! Madison thought. She couldn't read the rest. Bigwheels had totally gone off—the e-mail was over TWO PAGES long.

Madison scanned it to see if it ever mentioned anything aside from Reggie and his incredible cuteness.

The name Reggie appeared in every single sentence.

Madison heaved a frustrated sigh. She couldn't believe that Bigwheels hadn't even mentioned anything about Madison's dad and the jewelry store—or anything besides herself. It was like hearing from a different keypal.

She was about to hit REPLY, when Madison noticed her buddy list at the corner of the screen. Bigwheels was online.

Madison Insta-Messaged her.

<MadFinn>: Vicki! I need to talk to U
<Bigwheels>: HI! I'm so glad ur online! I wanted to tell you a funny story.
<MadFinn>: Is it about Reggie?
<Bigwheels>: Yes—why?
<MadFinn>: ur always talking about him
<Bigwheels>: I know I like him sooooo much
<MadFinn>: I don't even have a boyfriend.
<Bigwheels>: Im sorry
<MadFinn>: I'm not trying to be rude. It's just hard to always read ur love letters
<Bigwheels>: I never really thought about it
<MadFinn>: It's not that I don't want to hear about him at all . . . I just want to hear

about other stuff, too.
<Bigwheels>: Sorry if I got carried away
<MadFinn>: And I'm sorry if I sound harsh. . . . I just miss the old U. What happened to giving good advice?
<Bigwheels>: im so sorry Maddie
<MadFinn>: So—what do u mean by boyfriend, anyway?
<Bigwheels>: huh
<MadFinn>: I mean, is it all just talk? Or :-***? Or something else?
<Bigwheels>: No kissing yet. But I'm hoping for one (or two) at the dance.
<MadFinn>: Yeah, me too. LOL!
<Bigwheels>: u never know. how r things w/ur Dad
<MadFinn>: he isn't asking Stephanie to marry him.
<Bigwheels>: I knew he wouldn't without telling you first!!!
<MadFinn>: I have so much homework. TTYL?
<Bigwheels>: Definitely.
<MadFinn>: *poof*

Madison was relieved. Her keypal was back to normal, at least for now.

Twing!

Her computer chimed, signaling that another message had come in. Was it from Bigwheels again? Madison checked her inbox, and her eyes grew wider.

It was from Orange Crush!

She clicked on the message right away.

```
From: Orange Crush
To: MadFinn
Subject: Dance
Date: Wed 12 Feb 10:11 PM
```

```
I hope we can dance together this
Friday.

YSA
```

YSA, Madison thought. For, "Your Secret Admirer."

She sat back in her chair and folded her arms across her chest. Could the message really be from Drew? It was the kind of thing that someone might say after being turned down as a date. Wasn't it?

There was so much Madison didn't know—about Drew, valentines, and everything in between. She would have to keep reading the signs carefully.

The dance was only two days away.

Chapter 11

"Here you go, Ms. Finn," Mr. Books, the librarian, said as he handed Madison a book on the First Ladies of the American Revolution. Madison had hurried to the sixth-floor library the minute school was over. When Mr. Gibbons had asked everyone to discuss their paper topics in class, she and Fiona practically crawled under the desks. They HAD to do some real work—fast. Fiona was planning to meet Madison after soccer practice.

Mr. Books handed Madison some more useful materials.

"There is a good chapter on Abigail Adams in this text. And here is a book on both John and Abigail Adams, and another just on Abigail," he added,

pulling two more books down from the shelf. "I think you'll find a lot of useful information."

Madison's heart sank as he handed her three *more* thick books. There was no way she'd be able to read all of these today! "Um, thanks Mr. Books," she said, "but—do you have a book with their letters? That's really what I need."

"Sadly, no," Mr. Books said. "Have you tried looking on the Internet?"

Madison jerked her head toward her computer. "Yeah," she said. "But I could only find a couple of the letters. The entire collection isn't available online."

"Well," Mr. Books said, stroking his long chin thoughtfully, "have you tried the Far Hills library?"

Madison shook her head. "That's a great idea. Thanks, Mr. Books."

The librarian smiled. "Any time," he said.

Madison took her books back to her carrel and shoved them into her book bag. Her shoulders slumped with its weight. When Madison folded up her laptop and placed it inside, she felt like a turtle walking into the hallway. These biographies would come in handy, but right now they felt like boulders.

"Hey, Maddie!" a voice called as Madison stepped through the school's front door. "Wait up!"

Madison turned and saw Aimee chasing after her. Aimee ran like a dancer—each step seemed like an elegant leap. "Why aren't you at after-school ballet

practice?" Madison asked as her friend caught up to her. Aimee took ballet at Far Hills Junior High and at an outside studio in town.

"It was canceled," Aimee explained. "In fact, it's canceled for the rest of the week. The dance teacher has the flu."

"That's terrible," Madison said.

"Yeah," Aimee agreed. "I guess I'll have to put in some extra practice time at Madame Elaine's studio. Are you headed home? Let's walk together."

"Actually," Madison said, "I'm going to the town library."

Aimee lifted her eyebrows. "You're going to get *more* books?" she asked, staring at Madison's already-stuffed bag.

Madison laughed. "Just one more. Do you want to come?"

"Sure," Aimee said with a shrug. "I don't have anything better to do except homework. I just need to call my mom."

"Me too," Madison said as she and Aimee started walking toward the library. "We can use the pay phone at the library."

The Far Hills Town Library was the oldest building in town, and it was located just down the road from school. It was a beautiful old limestone building with tall Gothic towers, and—best of all—a stained-glass window that faced you as you walked in. As a little girl, Madison had called the library "the magic castle."

The front steps were slippery with ice, and Madison and Aimee had to hold on to the iron railing as they walked up to the heavy oak front door. Just inside, the wide gray doormat was soaked with ice and slush, some of which had melted over the slick marble floor. A yellow SLIPPERY WHEN WET sign stood nearby, the only evidence of modern times in sight. Madison looked up at the multicolored glass window, which glowed beautifully even in the dim February light, and wondered how long it had been since she had come here. At least two years, she guessed. Since before her parents split. Mom and Dad and Madison had used to come here together on weekends.

Now that she was here, Madison realized just how much she had missed the place.

Madison and Aimee descended a small set of stairs toward the phones and the rest rooms. Aimee called her mom and asked her to pick them up in half an hour. Then Madison left a message for her mom letting her know what time she'd be home.

The girls trooped up to the lobby and Madison walked up to the massive oak reference desk. A slim African American woman with small oval glasses was sitting there, leafing through an enormous volume.

"Excuse me," Madison said in a whisper. "I'm looking for the letters of John and Abigail Adams."

The librarian looked up at her and smiled. "That's

wonderful," she said warmly, as though Madison had chosen the best book in the whole library. "I'll show you where you can find them."

Madison gestured to Aimee, and the two girls followed the librarian through the main room, where an assortment of Far Hills residents sat at long tables, bent over books of all shapes and sizes. The librarian led them to a dim corner at the far end of the room. The shelves were lined with volume after volume, reaching all the way to the ceiling. Madison felt like they were the first people to visit that part of the magic castle in a long time.

"Let me see," the librarian said as she peered at the titles on the shelves. "I think you'll want the abridged version. That has only the best of the letters." As Madison watched the librarian's fingers trace along the spines of the books, she thought of her computer teacher, Mrs. Wing. Mrs. Wing always called herself a "cybrarian" when she helped her students with their online research. Madison thought about how different it was to look things up on the Internet. Even though you could search things more easily, sometimes the computer returned so many choices that it was hard to find what you were looking for. There was something nice about having a librarian who actually knew the books in the library, and could help you find what you wanted on the shelves.

Finally, the librarian found what she wanted. "Ah—here you are," she said, pulling the volume

from the shelf. "Enjoy," she said with a smile. "This should be very interesting reading."

Madison flipped open the book and started scanning the pages.

"What is that?" Aimee asked, peering into Madison's book. "Old letters, or something?"

"Yeah," Madison said. "John Adams was the second president of the United States, and the vice president under George Washington. He and his wife wrote a ton of letters. She kept begging him to give women rights, but he didn't listen to her."

"No kidding?" Aimee said as Madison took off her book bag and settled cross-legged on the floor. She pulled a random book off the shelf and flipped through it absently. "Abigail Adams should have given her husband a piece of her mind." She sat down next to Madison, and started to read.

Madison pulled out a small pad of purple Post-it notes and began to mark pages with the best letters. That way, she could show them to Fiona when she came over later.

"Hey, look at this," Aimee said, leaning over to show Madison her book. It was a collection of letters from lots of famous people.

"'I cannot exist without you—I am forgetful of every thing but seeing you again—my life seems to stop there—I see no further,'" Madison read aloud. "Who wrote that?"

"John Keats," Aimee said, reading from the

page. "He was a poet. It says here that he was in love with this woman named Fanny Brawne."

"Wow," Madison said. John Keats was way more romantic than John and Abigail Adams, that was for sure. She checked her watch. "We'd better get going," she said, dragging her bag back up over her shoulders. It seemed to weigh a ton. "Your mom will be here soon."

"Okay," Aimee said, sliding the book she was reading back into its place on the shelf. "This was fun. I have to come back here."

Madison and Aimee walked toward the front desk so that Madison could check out her book.

"Hey!" Aimee said. "There's Dan!" Sure enough, Dan was standing at the front desk, checking out books. Madison gulped. Standing right next to Dan was Hart Jones, looking cuter than ever in a navy blue cap and a gray parka.

Aimee hurried over to say hi.

"Aimee—stop!" Madison hissed, but Aimee didn't hear her. She had no choice but to follow.

"Hey, Dan! Hey, Hart!" Aimee said as she walked up to the counter.

Dan turned around and smiled at her. "Hey, look, it's Aimee—and an orange camel," he added, inspecting Madison's overstuffed backpack.

Madison wanted to disappear when Dan said that. She didn't want Hart to permanently associate her with a camel.

"Yeah, Finnster," Hart said with a grin. "Looks like you're doing a little bit of studying."

"Just a little bit," Madison said as the librarian scanned her book.

"Are you both ready for the dance Friday?" Dan asked. "I'm psyched to show off my moves." He did a little wiggle, and Aimee and Madison cracked up laughing. The four friends walked out of the library together.

"There's our ride," Dan said, indicating the car parked at the curb. Eileen waved from behind the wheel, and Madison waved back. "Do you need a lift?" Dan asked.

"No thanks," Aimee said. "My mom is picking us up."

"See you later, then," Hart said.

"See you," Madison and Aimee said as Hart and Dan climbed into the car. Eileen gave the horn a friendly little tap.

"Dan is so hilarious," Aimee said as the car pulled away.

"Yeah," Madison agreed.

But she wasn't thinking about Dan when she said it.

She was staring at the back of Hart's head in the rear window of the car as they drove away.

Orange Crush, Madison thought. I hope it's *you*.

Chapter 12

"You look great!" Aimee said as she and Madison walked into school on Friday.

Madison had curled her hair so that it was long and full. She'd applied some lip gloss, too, with an extra shimmer of seashell pink. Madison had on her favorite faded jeans and a black turtleneck sweater. Mom had loaned her a big, red heart pin, which she had attached to the sweater.

She had to look good at school now and at the dance later. Today was the day Orange Crush would reveal himself.

Aimee looked pretty, too. She wore a jean skirt with patches on it, including one that was shaped like a heart, and a long-sleeved pink T-shirt.

"Oh my God!" Aimee cried as they walked in the doors at school.

The building had erupted in a volcano of red, white, and pink. Halls were hung with streamers and banners advertising the Heart to Heart Dance, and everyone was dressed in Valentine's Day colors. Kids ran around, passing out valentine's cards and bags of candy.

Fiona spotted her BFFs and ran over. She was wearing a pink sweater set and cargo pants.

"Hey, Maddie!" she said. "I got your e-card—thanks!" Madison wasn't sure that paper valentines were a cool thing to send in junior high school, so she had sent all of her good friends e-cards.

Fiona handed one small envelope to Madison, and one to Aimee.

Madison pulled out her small card. On it was a picture of a bee in a mining hat. "Bee Mine," the card read. On the inside, Fiona had written,

Madison, I'm so glad that we've gotten to be good friends this year. I can't wait for us to have a blast at the dance! BFF 4-ever! Hearts and kisses, Fiona

Madison gave Fiona a giant hug. "Thanks," she said.

Aimee held up her card.

"Oh, Fiona, this is so totally sweet," Aimee said as

she finished reading her card. On the front was a picture of a little bear dressed up as a ballerina. The message read: VALENTINE, YOU'RE TUTU SWEET.

"Group hug!" Aimee squealed.

She wrapped her arms around Fiona and Madison, and pulled a Tupperware container out of a paper bag she was carrying.

"I wasn't sure if we were doing cards, or what, so I made cookies," she explained. "With all-natural honey and brown sugar, of course, courtesy of my Mom."

She lifted the lid and Madison and Fiona each took a heart-shaped sugar cookie covered with red sprinkles.

"Yum!" Madison said, taking a bite. "Breakfast!"

"Who brought cookies?" Egg asked, butting in. Drew and Chet were standing right behind him.

"Want one?" Aimee asked, offering the container to the guys, who—of course—didn't have to be asked twice. "Got enough, there, Chet?"

"I'm a growing boy," Chet said, holding up the three cookies he'd snatched. "I need to keep my strength up!"

Egg pulled a large red envelope out of his backpack.

"Uh . . . here," he said, handing the card to Fiona. "You can open it later."

Fiona blushed and stuffed it into her bag. "Okay," she whispered.

Madison couldn't believe that Egg had picked out a romantic card—and given it to Fiona right there in the hallway! Wow, they really *are* a couple, she thought.

Chet rolled his eyes and elbowed Egg in the side. He looked like he was about to say something sarcastic, but Drew stepped in quickly.

"Hey, I almost forgot," Drew interrupted. "I got us all tickets for the dance." He pulled the tickets out of his pocket. "It was cheaper to buy four sets of two so I just went ahead and got them," Drew explained. "I already gave Hart and Dan their tickets. Now you each owe me four bucks. Just pay me back at the dance."

"That was nice of you," Aimee said.

"Yeah, thanks," Egg said, grabbing two. He handed a ticket to Fiona.

"You didn't have to—" Madison said, a little perplexed.

"I know," Drew said. "But we're friends, so . . ."

"Weren't you going with someone else?" Chet asked Madison.

"Yeah, well, that fell through," Madison said, trying to cover for her excuse.

"Should we all just meet at the dance?" Drew asked, changing the subject.

"That's a good idea," Egg said. "I was thinking we could all show up in front at the same time and walk in together."

"Good idea," Fiona agreed. "Lindsay Frost told

me that she wants to come with us. She already has her ticket."

"And Ben, too," Aimee said, her voice lifting a little.

"Ben Buckley?" Egg said, making a face. He poked Aimee in the side. "With *you*?"

Aimee smirked. "Maybe . . ."

Madison and Fiona giggled.

"Does seven o'clock sound good to everyone?" Drew asked.

Madison grinned. Now the dance really was turning into a group thing. She'd spent all of that time worrying about being dateless for nothing. And Drew was being so nice.

All the suspects would be there—so Orange Crush was bound to reveal himself.

The bell rang, and Madison waved good-bye and headed off to the computer lab. She needed to do a quick spelling and grammar check on the paper she and Fiona worked on. They'd spent Thursday night working on their biography project for Mr. Gibbons. Madison had found all the letters from John Adams that they needed.

The lab was empty and Madison headed over to one of the computers and popped her disk into the drive. It didn't take long for her to correct the paper—there were only a few mistakes. She printed it out and stuffed the paper into her backpack. On the same disk, she opened a personal file she'd been working on.

Valentine's Day

Rude Awakening: This Valentine's Day dance is full of heart and soul for so many of my friends. But is it just heart and solo for me?

I've got less than five hours until the Valentine's Day dance—and I'm still dateless. Sigh. At least all of my friends will be there. And it looks as though they've decided not to pair off like animals on the ark.

I'm glad that I'll have my dad's digital camera. I can just roam around, and stay busy snapping photos. I can't wait to see everyone all dressed up. I wonder what the guys will wear? Maybe Egg will show up in a tuxedo. HA!

My only consolation is that I'm probably not the only person who's dateless. As far as I know, Hart doesn't have a date. So maybe he *will* ask me to dance with him when we get there?

If he does I think I'll have a heart attack. Or is that a Hart attack? LOL.

Madison closed her file, and looked at the clock above Mrs. Wing's desk. She still had ten minutes before the bell, so she decided to write to Bigwheels, too. She'd save the message and send it later.

```
From: MadFinn
To: Bigwheels
Subject: Hi!
Date: Fri 14 Feb 8:35 AM
```

```
Just wanted to say Happy Valentine's
Day! I hope I wasn't too strange
when we chatted the other night.
I've just been going through this
kind of insecure phase because it
seems like everyone around me is
totally in love, including YOU. And
I'm not. N e way, I want you to
know that I don't mind hearing
about Reggie. I'm glad that you're
so psyched. I'm psyched 4 u.

Yours till the Hershey's kisses,

Madison
```

Madison felt better just writing down her apology to Bigwheels. She needed to be more understanding. After all, Madison wrote about Hart in practically every e-mail and Bigwheels only ever had good things to say. And Bigwheels always gave the best advice whenever Madison had other problems or questions, too.

Madison hit SAVE just as the bell rang. She popped out the disk and headed down the hall toward her science class.

"Hello, Madison," Ivy said with a smug little smile

as Madison took her seat beside her lab partner. "Ready for the dance?" Ivy was wearing a tight red sweater with a black skirt, and her fingernails had little heart decals on them.

"I guess," Madison said. She didn't feel like talking to Ivy, but didn't want to be rude, either.

"I can't wait to go," Ivy went on, giving her hair a flip. "It should be so much fun—Hart and I are going together. Isn't that great?"

Madison glared at Ivy.

Was it true? Had Hart really asked Ivy to the dance?

Just then, he strolled into the classroom, trailing a silver balloon in the shape of a heart. He looked around the classroom. When he spotted Madison, he waved.

He's coming this way, Madison thought. Time seemed to slow down as Hart approached. Is he bringing that balloon to *me*?

Madison had to grip the edge of the lab table to steady herself.

Every detail of Hart's face seemed cuter than ever. Madison took in his dimples, the slight spray of freckles across his nose, the way the light shone on his hair . . .

"Finnster," Hart said as he walked up to her. "This is for you."

Madison opened her mouth to speak. No words came out.

On the other side of Madison, Ivy groaned.

"Uh . . . but the thing is . . . it's not from me," Hart added.

"W-w-what?" Madison asked.

Madison stared at him for a moment. It was as though he had spoken to her in a foreign language—her brain simply refused to understand what he had just said. It wasn't from him?

"Someone asked me to give it to you," Hart explained.

Hart handed Madison the balloon, and she wrapped its string around her wrist.

"Yeah, someone asked me," Hart said with an enormous smile on his face. "There's a note, I think." He pointed to a small white envelope. A hole had been punched in the corner. It was tied to the balloon.

Madison pulled out the card. It was typed, just like the others.

You've got my heart on a string.
Tonight all will be revealed.

signed, Your Secret Admirer.

Madison blushed, confused.

Hart smiled again. "It's nice, huh?" he said.

Madison smiled back. "Yeah. Who is it from?"

Hart stalled. "I can't reveal my sources."

Madison crinkled her eyebrows in deep thought.

Had Hart just pretended the balloon was from someone else to throw Madison off his trail? He still could be Orange Crush . . . right?

"Uh, Ivy," Hart said, "my mom says that if you still need that ride to the dance, we'll have to pick you up at seven. She's got her book group tonight."

"For sure," Ivy said, nodding. "I have to be there early to help set up, anyway."

Madison stared over at Ivy, who snapped, "I told you Hart and I are going to the dance."

"Right," Madison said. Now she knew the real story. Ivy and Hart *were* going to the dance together—but not in the way that Ivy had first implied.

"See you at the dance, too, Finnster?" Hart said as he turned toward his own lab table.

Madison's bit her lip to keep from screaming.

WHAT IS GOING ON? WHY CAN'T HE JUST ADMIT THAT HE'S ORANGE CRUSH?

"Nice balloon. So who sent it to you?" Ivy asked. "Egg?"

"Very funny," Madison said. She nodded in the direction of Hart. "I think you know who sent this to me, Ivy."

"You don't really think that balloon is from Hart," Ivy said nastily. "Not in this lifetime, Madison. He just told you it was from someone else!"

Madison didn't respond to that remark. She turned and tied the balloon to the back of her chair.

Of course she *did* think the balloon was from

Hart. He was being sneakier than sneaky, that's all.

And tonight all would be revealed once and for all.

Ivy just wishes Hart had given the balloon to *her*, Madison thought. She laughed quietly from behind her science textbook.

Not in this lifetime, Poison Ivy.

Chapter 13

"Smile!" Madison said as she aimed the digital camera at Aimee and Fiona. Her BFFs wrapped their arms around each other and grinned as Madison snapped the photo. They were standing in front of a giant heart-shaped cutout that the student council had put up next to the entrance to the gym.

"Dan," Madison said. "Would you take one of all of us?"

"Hey!" Dan protested. "What am I? Wallpaper?"

"She meant all of us *girls*, Dan," Aimee said, punching him on the shoulder. It was 6:55. Madison's mom had brought the girls a little early, since she had to chaperone. Dan's mom, Eileen, had done the same thing.

"Hold it," Dan said, reaching for the camera.

"Oh, no," Lindsay said, reddening a little. "I always hate pictures of myself."

"But you look nice," Dan said. Lindsay struck a pose and grinned. Madison could tell that Dan's compliment had really made her happy. She was normally super shy, but in her red velvet dress, Lindsay looked special tonight. The deep red set off her blond hair and made her pale skin glow.

"Everybody say, 'Cheesy!'" Dan said as he snapped the photo.

"Madison, I just love your little tiara," Lindsay said.

"Thanks," Madison said. She'd almost decided not to wear it, but Aimee and Fiona had talked her into it at the last minute. Now she was glad that she had. This was the third compliment she'd gotten tonight.

"Here we are, the fun can start now," said a voice behind them.

They all turned to see Egg, followed by Drew, Ben, and Chet. When Egg saw Fiona, he stopped in his tracks. Madison giggled. It wasn't often that she saw Egg speechless. Not that Madison blamed him. Fiona looked great in a hot-pink tank paired with a bright orange skirt. Both were made of raw silk, and shimmered slightly under the lights.

"I didn't know it was possible for you to look that good," Chet said to his sister.

"Well it *is* hard, considering that we share the same DNA," Fiona shot back. Then she turned to Egg. "You look very nice, Walter," she said.

"Thanks," Egg said. He held his hands out like he wanted to give her a compliment. "You, too."

"Okay, so now we're all here," Aimee said, looking around. "What are we waiting for? Let's go in."

The friends headed toward the entrance to the gym, where there was a table set up. Since she was class president and chair of the dance committee, Ivy sat there taking tickets along with representatives from the eighth and ninth grades, too. Two girls checked everyone's name against a list and handed out the carnations. Madison knew one of them, Monica Jennings, from her English class. She always hung around with the older kids.

"Nice tiara, Madison," Ivy sneered as she took Madison's ticket. Ivy was wearing a tiara, too, only it was much larger and had clear pink stones instead of blue.

"Same to you," Madison said, trying as hard as she could to be polite. "Do you have to sit here all night?"

Ivy rolled her eyes. "Just for half an hour," she said. "We're taking turns."

"Where's your date?" Madison asked.

Ivy cocked her head to one side and flipped her hair. "Around," she said.

Madison's stomach flip-flopped. She couldn't wait to see him.

"Madison Finn?" Monica asked, reading Madison's name off the carnation list.

"Yes?" Madison said, turning around.

"Someone sure likes you," Monica said. She counted out fifteen carnations and handed them to Madison. They made an enormous bouquet.

"For me?" Madison asked eagerly. "From who?"

"No clue," Monica said with a shrug. "Whoever bought them didn't include a message."

Aimee lifted her eyebrows knowingly at Madison, who blushed. The mystery continues, Madison thought.

But it meant Orange Crush was there.

Ivy pretended that she hadn't seen what happened. "Next!" she cried, looking toward the next seventh graders who were walking into the dance.

As Madison and her friends turned, a pack of ninth-grade boys walked out of the gym, and a blast of music escaped through the open door, then faded as the door swung closed behind them.

"Wow, sounds pretty good in there," Dan said. "Let's go!"

It took a moment for Madison's eyes to adjust to the dim light, but she could see that the gym was already pretty crowded. As she looked around, Madison had to admit that Ivy and the rest of the student council had done a great job decorating the

gym. With the lights dimmed and the walls covered in silver and red balloons and streamers, the gym looked . . . well, *romantic*.

They headed over to the bleachers and tossed their coats into a heap. Madison laid her carnations on top of her little purse as she set it down gently on the floor of the bleachers.

"So, are you guys ready to dance, or what?" Fiona asked.

"I could dance," Egg said. Madison couldn't help smiling when she looked at him. This was the first time she had *ever* seen Egg in a tie. He looked sort of uncomfortable in it—but he looked nice, too. The tie had smiley faces on it, and some of them were sticking out their tongues. "Anyone else want to?" Egg asked.

"Not yet," Ben said. "I think I want to get some punch. Want some, Aimee?"

"Sure thing," Aimee said, beaming. She'd worn her favorite pink slip dress and shimmery stockings. Her hair was braided and piled on top of her head. Her "date" seemed to like it.

Ben, Chet, and Drew went to check out the snack table. Madison looked over and waved at Mom, who was working as a chaperone and manning the soda bar with Señora Diaz. Mom waved back, smiling. The snack zone was set up near the rear entrance to the gym. Students weren't supposed to take plates and cups out of the zone, but when Madison looked

around, she saw that the rule wasn't being enforced. Half of the kids on the dance floor had a cup in their hand.

"Would you like to dance, Lindsay?" Dan asked.

Moments before, Lindsay had looked sadder than sad when she discovered she was the only one of the girls who hadn't gotten a carnation. But now she brightened up. "Dance? That would be great!" she said.

She and Dan followed Egg and Fiona onto the dance floor.

"Dan's a cool guy," Aimee said as she watched him dance with Lindsay.

"Definitely," Madison agreed. "He and Lindsay make a cute couple."

"Check out Egg and Fiona," Aimee grunted.

Madison laughed. A slow song was playing, and Egg and Fiona had their arms around one another as they swayed slowly to the music. Fiona was a little taller than Egg, and she was resting her cheek against the top of his head. Her eyes were closed and she looked really happy.

"They look like they're in love," Aimee said.

Love? For a moment, Madison was about to tell Aimee not to talk crazy. But when she looked at Egg and Fiona again, she had to admit that it did look that way, like in a movie.

Ben came over and sat down next to Aimee.

"No drink?" Aimee asked.

"They're out of ice," Ben said. "Drew and Chet are waiting for it, but I figured I'd just go back later." He leaned back and looked at Aimee. "So—are you ready to show off some of your ballerina moves?" he asked.

"Why, did you bring your toe shoes?" Aimee shot back.

Ben stood up, gave a deep bow, and said, "May I have this dance?"

"Well, I guess so," Aimee said. "I did get all dressed up—"

Ben headed toward the dance floor, and Aimee turned to Madison. "Do you mind if I go dance for a little while?" Aimee whispered. "Will you be okay?"

Her friend looked so eager, Madison had to smile. She knew Aimee really wanted to dance, but Madison was grateful that her friend cared enough to make sure that she was okay. "Don't worry about me," Madison said. "Besides, Drew and Chet are coming back soon. No big."

"Thanks," Aimee said, giving Madison a little hug. Then she joined Ben, who was waiting for her at the edge of the dance floor.

Madison watched Aimee dance with Ben. The music had changed to a quicker beat, and Aimee twirled around more and more as she got into the music. Little blond wisps of her hair fell down and framed her face as she bobbed her head to the beat. She looked pretty.

Madison took her Dad's camera out of her purse. She walked around the dance floor, snapping photos here and there. She tried to get pictures of everyone. It was strange to be snapping photos of eighth and ninth graders who she didn't know, but everyone grinned at Madison when she pointed to the camera and shouted "FAR HILLS!" over the music.

Once Madison had been around the dance floor once, she went back to her seat on the bleachers. There were two half-empty soda cups there, so she guessed that Drew and Chet had finally bought their drinks and then wandered away again. She crossed her legs and looked around.

The DJ had a fog machine that was just starting to release a cloud of fragrant gray smoke over the crowd. Madison noticed that most of the people were dancing in big groups now, not in couples. Dan and Lindsay had been joined by a group of girls from the volleyball team, and they had all made a huge circle. Lindsay was smiling and clapping her hands. Madison was tempted to join them.

"Hey, Finnster."

Madison looked up at Hart. His eyes looked even deeper green than usual and he looked handsomer than handsome in a black button-down shirt and a red tie. Madison caught her breath as he sat down next to her on the bleachers.

"Some party, huh?" Hart said.

"Y-y-yeah," Madison stammered. Hart must have

been wearing some kind of cologne, because he smelled warm and spicy.

"Good DJ," Hart remarked. He turned to face Madison. As he grinned, his dimples deepened in his face. "Have you been out on the dance floor yet?"

Madison couldn't speak. Was Hart going to ask her to dance?

Hart's smile widened. "Well, do you—"

"Hey, I'm glad we found you guys," Chet said as he raced over to them. Drew was right behind him. "You're not going to believe what's happening!"

Madison felt her stomach flip-flop.

Why were Chet and Drew here *now*? She was certain that Hart was about to ask her to dance! Why did boys have to have such lousy timing?

"What's going on?" Hart asked.

"A seventh grader was found in Mr. Danehy's lab," Drew whispered. "She got caught by a hall chaperone."

"Yeah, and the best part," Chet said, "is that she was making out with a ninth grader."

"No way," Madison gasped. "In the science lab?"

"It's totally true," Drew said. "Some lab experiment, huh?" he said, cracking a bad joke.

"Wow," Hart said, "Who was the seventh grader?"

"I haven't heard yet," Chet said. "But I'm going to see who knows." He rushed out onto the dance floor and tapped Dan on the shoulder.

Madison, Drew, and Hart scanned the dance

floor to see if they could figure out who the trouble-makers were. Madison didn't see Ivy anywhere. Was it *her*? She imagined how great it would be if Poison Ivy Daly got busted at the dance that she herself had planned.

The news of the science lab soon reached everyone in the room. Everyone on the dance floor was gossiping instead of dancing. Except for Fiona and Egg. They were still swaying to the music, lost in goo-goo land.

"What's this about a seventh grader getting caught with a ninth grader?" Aimee asked as she hurried over.

"You know as much as we do," Madison said.

"I heard that the guy had his shirt off," Ben put in.

"Okay, you know *more* than we do," Madison said. "What were they doing?"

"Kissing," Ben said. "I heard that the girl's hair was all messed up."

"That doesn't sound like such a big deal," Hart said.

Fiona and Egg came over. Madison noticed that they were holding hands now. "Hi," Fiona said, dreamily. Egg just grinned.

"Wow, those kids are going to be in so much trouble," Madison said.

"Who?" Egg asked.

"Where have you *been*?" Chet said. "The seventh

grader and the ninth grader who got caught making out!"

"They could get suspended for this," Madison said.

"Definitely," Hart agreed. "Principal Bernard is going to freak, especially after he made up that huge list of rules for us to sign."

"Okay, I found out who it was," Chet said as he ran up to them. He was panting a little, and had to take a couple of deep breaths. "It was Zeke Christian and Monica Jennings."

"Monica?" Aimee said. "You mean Carnation Girl?"

"Isn't Zeke that guy who hangs out on the ninth grade corner, sometimes?" Madison asked. The ninth grade corner was where the coolest ninth graders liked to hang out before and after school. At least, *they* thought they were the coolest.

"That's him," Drew said.

"Unbelievable," Madison said. Personally, Madison would never have thought that Monica would go for a greasy guy like Zeke. But it was no surprise that she was with someone older.

"I'm glad I don't have to explain that one to my parents," Aimee whispered in Madison's ear. "But don't you think Zeke is kind of cute?"

"Tell me you're kidding," Madison said.

Suddenly, the music stopped. But the whole room was buzzing with the sound of junior-high schoolers trading gossip.

Principal Bernard walked up to the DJ table and took the microphone. "Everyone, may I have your attention?" he said. Everyone covered their ears as the microphone let out a small shriek of feedback. "Uh—sorry about that," the principal said as he held the mic a bit further from his mouth. "I just wanted to let everyone know that there was a 'situation' earlier, but it has been resolved, with many thanks to our parent chaperone, Josselyn Kenyon."

"Phony Joanie's mom," Aimee whispered to Madison, who shook her head and giggled.

"Oh, man. I'm so glad *my* mom didn't bust them," Madison said. "She would have been on my case for days."

"I also wanted to let everyone know that our school has already raised almost three thousand five hundred dollars for the International Heart Society," Principal Bernard continued. "So, please give yourselves and the members of the student council a round of applause."

"Wow, that's a ton of money," Madison said.

"I hate to admit it, but Ivy did a great job," Aimee agreed.

Everyone clapped. Then the music started up again.

"Hey, Ben," Aimee said. "You want to go back out on the dance floor?"

"Definitely," Ben said.

Fiona and Egg went to dance again, too. Chet

left to see if he could round up any more gossip about Zeke and Monica.

Madison tucked a piece of hair behind her ear and looked in Hart's direction.

That was when *she* walked up.

"Hart, I've been looking all over for you," Ivy said as she wrapped her arm around Hart's. She didn't even look in Madison's direction. "I'm ready for my dance now."

"Oh," Hart said. "I'll see you later, Madison, okay?"

Madison forced herself to smile at him as she was left there, standing alone with Drew.

Now Madison had no idea what to say. Drew wasn't talking either.

Was Hart her mysterious admirer—or not? Had he planned to ask her to dance in the first place—or not? Was Drew ever going to talk to her again—or not?

Madison snuck a look at Drew out of the corner of her eye. He had been looking at her, but he looked away when she glanced at him. Had Drew been her secret admirer all along? She hadn't even given him a chance.

Madison had to know *now*. Once and for all—who was Orange Crush?

There was only one way to find out.

Chapter 14

Madison turned and faced Drew.

She couldn't ask a question like *Have you been sending me secret poems?*, so she decided to try another approach.

"Hey," Madison said. "Having fun?"

Drew gave her a lopsided half-smile. "Yeah. That's a nice dress you have on," he said awkwardly.

"Thanks," Madison said.

Drew glanced away.

"I like your flowers, too," she said. Madison hoped that once she had thanked Drew for the carnations, he would admit that he had sent them.

"Flowers?" Drew asked. "Oh—you mean these?" he said, holding out his tie. It was covered with

bright splotches of color. "I think they're just blobs, actually."

"Oh," Madison said, confused. "Well, not exactly." She took a deep breath. "Look, Drew, there's something I've been wanting to say to you."

Drew lifted his eyebrows. "Yeah?"

Madison bit her lip. "I'm really sorry about the way I acted—when you asked me to the dance."

"Oh, that," Drew said. He shrugged. "No biggie. I'm over it. We're friends again. That's cool."

Madison blinked. *Over it?* But if he was over it, why would he have sent an e-mail saying that he hoped they could dance together?

He wouldn't have.

Which meant that he really wasn't her secret admirer.

"Of course," Madison said. "We're friends."

"I think I'm going to get some nachos," Drew said. "You want anything?"

Madison shook her head, and Drew wandered over toward the snack table. Madison looked up at the giant clock on the wall of the gym. It was already eight thirty. She had expected to spend the evening dancing with her secret admirer, but now she was starting to wonder if her mystery boy really had been a prank, after all.

Madison gazed across the room and saw Dan standing on the side of the dance floor. She wandered over to say hello. Dan was good at cheering

her up. He could take her mind off of all of this secret-admirer stuff.

"Hey, Dan," Madison said, tapping him on the shoulder.

"Madison!" Dan said. "You scared me! Are you having fun?"

"Yeah," Madison said halfheartedly.

"What's wrong?" Dan asked. "You look a little down."

Madison shrugged. She didn't feel like explaining right now. "I'm fine," she lied. "The dance is great."

"Sure—" Dan agreed, "it's got everything, good music, good food, people making out and getting busted—"

Madison laughed.

"I can't wait to see Mr. Danehy's face on Monday morning," Dan went on, "when he finds out that his science lab was a major *love shack*."

Madison laughed again.

"He'll probably start padlocking his door from now on," Madison said.

"Maybe he won't let us into the room anymore," Dan suggested. "We'll all have to learn science in the hallway."

Madison giggled. "You're so funny," she said.

Dan smiled at her, then looked out at the dancers. "Did you get my e-mail?"

Madison nodded. "Yeah," she said, thinking for a moment about the one that he had sent her from

the Far Hills Animal Clinic. But that didn't make sense—he'd sent that on Tuesday. Why would he be asking about it now?

"No, wait," Madison said, shaking her head. "What e-mail?"

Dan looked at her, then cleared his throat. "Actually, I sent you a couple. . . . " he said. "Did you—did you get my poem?"

Madison's brain felt fuzzy. "Your poem?" she repeated. Her voice was barely above a whisper.

"I'm pretty sure you got the balloon," Dan went on, "and I *know* that you got the carnations. I was standing right behind you when you picked them up tonight."

"You?" Madison said.

All at once, the fog-machine air of the gym seemed to press down on her, and Madison struggled for breath.

She didn't know what to say.

She wanted to run.

"Excuse me," Madison whispered. "I'll be . . . right back . . ."

Madison took a step away from Dan, and then another, and soon she was running—running toward the exit as fast as she could. She could hear Dan calling her name, but Madison didn't look back.

She couldn't face him. She just couldn't.

Madison burst through the heavy gym door, and sucked in the icy February air deep into her lungs.

The cold air felt good on her skin, and she felt better as the door swung closed behind her and the music faded away.

Suddenly, deep sobs welled up from inside. Madison gave into them, her shoulders shaking. She wasn't sure why she was crying. She was shivering, but she couldn't tell whether it was from the cold or not. She didn't feel cold. Her nose started to run.

A blast of music cut through the still night air as the gym door swung open.

"Madison?" Mom called. "Honey bear?"

Mom came over, opened her coat, and drew Madison into a warm hug. She didn't say anything, just rubbed Madison's back as she had when Madison fell and skinned her knee as a little girl.

Madison sniffled and stopped shaking. "I . . . I think I drooled on your coat," she said finally. "I'm sorry."

Mom laughed. "Please," she said. "I've already spilled five different kinds of soda on myself. A little drool won't make any difference."

Mom brushed the tears away from Madison's cheeks with her palms.

"Do you want to talk?" Mom asked gently.

Madison shook her head. "I don't know why I'm freaking out—" She started, but she felt a lump grow in her throat. She had to swallow hard before she could go on. "It's just," she said in a whisper, "I just found out who my secret admirer is. It's Dan."

"Dan Ginsburg?" Mom asked. "That nice boy?"

Madison nodded.

"I see," Mom said softly. "But you thought it was . . . someone else."

Madison nodded again. Then her vision blurred and hot tears came spilling down her cheeks. "Oh, man," she whispered fiercely, "how could I have been so *stupid*?"

Mom hugged her again and kissed her head. "It's okay, sweetie," she said. "It's okay."

"What am I supposed to do?" Madison wailed. "Dan told me, and I ran away like an idiot. Now he probably hates me."

"I'm sure that he didn't go from liking you to hating you in five seconds," Mom said.

"You should have seen his face, Mom," Madison said.

"Well, I'm sure his feelings were hurt," Mom admitted. "But—isn't Dan a friend of yours?"

"Yes," Madison said, swiping at her tears. "So?"

"So—friends have fights," Mom explained. "And friends apologize and make up."

Madison stared at the ground. "I can't face him," she said. "I *can't*. I'll die."

Mom put her hand beneath Madison's chin and raised her face so that they were looking each other in the eye. "Madison, I know that you're embarrassed," she said gently. "And I know that you're disappointed that your secret admirer isn't who you thought it was.

But Dan is a good friend. And I think you know how hard it can be to have a crush on someone, especially if they may not feel the same way."

Madison swallowed hard. Mom was right.

"All right," Madison said finally. "I'll go back and talk to him." She wiped her face and looked up at her mom. "Do I look okay?" she asked.

Mom smoothed a lock of hair away from Madison's face. "Okay? Maddie, you look beautiful," she said.

Madison squeezed her Mom. "Thank you so much," she said.

"Now, let's get inside—I'm freezing!" Mom replied.

"Yeah, it is cold out here!" Madison agreed, folding her arms across her chest and shivering. The warm air greeted them as they walked back into the gym. Mom gave Madison's hand a little tug and returned to her chaperoning position by the soda table. Aimee and Ben were standing there, sipping Cokes.

"Have you guys seen Dan?" Madison asked them.

"No," Aimee said. She leaned over to Madison and out of Ben's earshot. "Maddie, are you okay? Have you been crying?"

"I'll tell you later," Madison said breathlessly. She stood on tiptoe and searched the room for Dan. He was standing by the bleachers, putting on his coat.

Madison hurried over as he started for the gym doors.

"Dan," she called out. "Wait."

Dan turned toward her, but he kept his eyes on the floor. Even in the dim light, Madison could see that his face was burning. He didn't say anything.

"Dan, I'm so sorry," Madison said in a rush. "I didn't mean to flip out. It's just that—you caught me by surprise."

Dan finally looked up at her, but she couldn't read the expression in his dark eyes.

"I mean, looking back on it, I guess I should have known that Orange Crush was you, but I didn't, and then when you said that it was you, I was just like, 'Wow, I had no clue,' and . . . and . . . and this is the part where you stop me from babbling," Madison said.

Dan gave her a little lopsided grin.

"Please," Madison went on. "Say something. Say *anything*."

Dan sighed. "I didn't mean to get you angry or sad," he said finally. "I'm really sorry if I embarrassed you."

"No—no," Madison said. "*I'm* sorry. It's not you. It's just that I'm not—I can't deal with this whole boyfriend thing right now."

Madison wished that this moment could be perfectly scripted like in the movies, where everyone always knows exactly what to say.

"I really like you, Dan," Madison continued.

"But as a friend," Dan said. "Right?"

"Yeah," Madison said. "A good friend."

"As a friend," Dan repeated. He looked at her a moment. "Well," he said slowly, "that's cool."

"Cool?" Madison asked. Her heart thudded in her chest.

"It's cooler than cool," Dan said slyly. Madison laughed to hear him use one of her expressions. "We have a lot in common, you know?"

"Like the animal shelter?" Madison asked.

Dan nodded. "And—you know—we both like peanut butter," he added.

Madison giggled. "And pizza."

"Yeah," Dan said with a grin. "Tons of stuff in common." He jammed his fists in his pockets and looked at the floor. "I just wanted to do something nice for you. You deserve it."

Madison touched Dan lightly on the shoulder. "You're the best," she said.

Behind them, the colored lights dimmed, and soft strains of slow music floated toward the ceiling.

"Well," Dan said uncomfortably, "I guess I'd better get going." He looked over his shoulder toward the door.

"No—wait," Madison said. "Don't you—do you want to dance?"

"Dance?" Dan said.

Madison bobbed up and down. "Yes, dance—with me," she said.

"I'd love to," Dan said. He dropped his coat on the bleachers and followed Madison onto the crowded dance floor.

Madison put her hands on Dan's shoulders and he put his hands at her waist, and they swayed to the soft music. Madison could see Fiona and Egg standing off to the side. Aimee and Ben were dancing, too, as were Ivy and Hart. Ivy had her head on Hart's chest and her eyes were closed, but Hart didn't really seem to be paying attention. He looked over at Madison as if to say *Hey!*

"So—Dan," Madison said, "can I still keep the balloon? And the flowers?"

Dan laughed. "I guess so," he said. "But I want the chocolate rose back."

"Oh, no," Madison said in mock horror. "I already ate it."

"*Ate* it?" Dan pretended to be shocked.

"Actually, I ate half of it," Madison admitted. "Aimee ate the other half."

"Well," Dan said slowly, "I guess you can keep it, then." He looked at Madison, his eyes twinkling. "But I just want you to know that I'm going to keep on liking you."

Madison was grateful for the darkness, because she knew that she was blushing furiously. "All right," she said finally as the disco ball spun colored light across the ceiling. "I guess that's a pretty fair deal."

The Dance

Mom and I just got home from the dance. Dad left a message on the answering machine earlier tonight from him and Stephanie both. I think I'm getting used to the idea of them being together. They wished me "good luck and surprising romance" tonight. Isn't that nice? If only they knew how right they were!!!

Rude Awakening: Love is definitely blind. I didn't see this one coming at all.

To think—all this time, Orange Crush was Dan Ginsburg—and I never even suspected it. My secret admirer really put the "Dan" in dance, ha-ha.

In some ways, I'm kind of relieved that my SA wasn't Hart. I mean, sure, it would have been amazing, and perfect and everything. But it also would have been a ton of pressure. The truth is, I'm not really sure that I'm ready to be in major love right now. Someday I will be, but not right now. I'll know the signs—I hope.

When Mom and I first got home, we took Phin for a long walk. (He was waiting for us all night!) He kept looking around on the street, for Peaches, I think. But he didn't seem too disappointed that the golden wasn't there. Even dogs have to get over their crushes.

I have been looking for all these

positive signs for romance. And I hope time will erase what happened w/Dan and Drew before and during the dance. I want to go on being normal friends just like always.

After all, friendship is the most important thing, right?

Mad Chat Words:

(:-...	Brokenhearted
:)~	Drooling
:-1K-	Long dress/prom dress
:-***	Smooches
IYD	In your dreams
FYA	For your amusement
MWBRL	More will be revealed later
DBEYH	Don't believe everything you hear
HTH	Hope this helps
OMG	Oh my god/Oh my gosh
R?	Really?
SYS	See you soon
WCA	Who cares, anyway?

Madison's Computer Tip

I was so excited when I got my first "signed, your secret admirer" e-mail. It was flattering to have someone say that he liked me. But even though it turned out that my "admirer" was someone friendly who I knew, I should have told Mom or Dad about the notes. I have to remember to be safe when I'm chatting or e-mailing on-line. What if the messages had been from a cyber phony? I've seen scary stories about them on the news. **If you are getting e-mails from strangers, you should hit DELETE and tell your parents.** Better to be safe than sorry, as Gramma Helen would say.

Visit Madison @ www.madisonfinn.com